THE
WATER LILY
WARRIORS

A NOVEL OF SENIOR SURVIVAL

D.A. FRANCIS

PERMUTED
PRESS

A PERMUTED PRESS BOOK
ISBN: 978-1-68261-930-8
ISBN (eBook): 978-1-68261-931-5

The Water Lily Warriors:
A Novel of Senior Survival
© 2020 by D.A. Francis
All Rights Reserved

Cover art by Angie @ Pro_ebookcovers
Back cover photo courtesy of Owen Waggoner

PERMUTED
PRESS

Permuted Press, LLC
New York • Nashville
permutedpress.com

Published in the United States of America

This novel is dedicated to Alice Walsh,
a delightful lady who is ninety-eight years young this year.
Her mind is sharp as a tack, and she is a font of wisdom to all
who have been fortunate enough to know her.
Alice was an actual witness to many of the climatic events of
the twentieth century which the rest of us can only read about
in history books. She is indeed one of my heroes.

CONTENTS

INTRODUCTION

In April of 2008 a report commissioned by the United States Congress was delivered to that body and the President. The title of the report was:

> *"Report of the Commission to Assess the Threat to the United States from Electromagnetic Pulse (EMP) Attack"*

The document is over two hundred pages in length, and details what would probably occur if the United States was successfully attacked, using nuclear weapons detonated in a near Earth orbit over our country. Currently, numerous low orbit satellites launched by potential adversaries like China, North Korea and Russia pass over our country many times a day. We don't know what they contain. Due to their continuing missile and nuclear development programs, it is entirely possible that Iran will join this group in the near future. The report is available online at:

www.empcommission.org

In a worst-case scenario, the commission estimated that due to a total breakdown of infrastructure, including food and medical supply distribution mechanisms, the failure of water treatment and supply facilities, and the near total loss of the electrical grid, would create a situation where *over ninety percent of the population could be dead within a year.* There is no indication that the report was taken seriously by the George W. Bush Administration or the Obama Administration which followed. Our major infrastructure, including the national power grid, is largely unprotected.

This book examines how a group of senior citizens in Happy Valley, a fictional large retirement community in South Carolina's Low Country, have fared in the year following such an event, and what they will have to do if they wish to continue to survive in an unimaginably threatening environment. I have included a glossary of terms which may be unfamiliar to the average reader.

PROLOGUE

THE EATER

I can see a man walking down Happy Valley Boulevard. A few months ago, I wouldn't have, because trees would have obscured my view. They're all gone now, chopped down for fuel or to make defensive barricades.

From my platform on the roof I can see that there is something wrong with him. He's too far away to determine what, but I can guess. We've seen a lot like him in the last few weeks. It's not a Zombie Apocalypse, but a group of people driven mad by hunger and the things they have done because of it. They have become cannibals, feeding off the bodies of the dead. We now refer to them as "Eaters of the Dead", from a book of that title some of us had read in the past. They are insane, and they are definitely dangerous.

None of the twenty members of the Water Lily Warriors, which is what we have come to call ourselves, could have imagined how bad it could really get if our country was the victim of an EMP attack. That had to be what happened, but we can't confirm it because all forms of electronic communication suddenly ceased in the middle of the night while we all were sleeping, almost a year ago today. Some of us were at least partially prepared, but most were not. Of the original eighty-six residents of our Water Lily neighborhood, only twenty are left, my wife and I among them. Some died from lack of their prescription medications, others from heart attacks or strokes, and sadly, not a few by suicide. The majority were victims of violent attacks by those initially looking for valuables, and later for food and water.

Some of us pooled our food and resources. Others refused to do so, and were thus on their own. They are all gone, left to the not so tender mercies of the looters who descended on our retirement community almost immediately after the attack. Those of us who were armed fought them off. We selected four contiguous houses and built defensive platforms on their roof as well as a spiked barricade around a large perimeter.

The youngest member of our group is sixty-four. I am the oldest at seventy-six. Some of us have useful skills to contribute. Others do not, but have become our worker bees, tending our garden, hauling water and chopping and splitting wood for our cooking fires. We badly need them and are grateful for their contribution to our survival.

In the first months of our ordeal we had to maintain an armed guard at all four corners of our compound twenty-four hours a day. Now we only have two on the roofs at night. The lack of vitamin A for the looters and eaters makes most of them almost totally night blind, and as such not a threat after dark. With the first rays of dawn, the full guard is mounted, and I am at the southeastern post this afternoon, equipped with binoculars and my scope mounted AR-15 rifle.

As I watch the stranger come closer, his features come into view. Dirty and disheveled, he is wearing what were probably expensive shoes, now scuffed and worn. His clothes consist of what appear to be dress grey slacks and a white short sleeved shirt. Both are in tatters. Curiously, on his wrist is a large, expensive looking watch. Rolex maybe? But the giveaway is the front of his shirt. It is stained brownish red with blood, and that is caked on his beard as well. He is definitely an "Eater" and must be dealt with before he comes closer.

At about three-hundred yards I have a clear shot and take it. He falls like a sack of cement. I watch intently through my scope, but he doesn't move, and a pool of blood soon surrounds his body. Not worth another shot to the head. The Turkey Vultures, which we call the Happy Valley Greeters, circle overhead. They will clean up the mess in a few days' time.

A greater concern has arisen. Although we have done all in our power to ration our food, water and medical supplies, they are absolutely finite, and will eventually be depleted. There is another consideration. Our human waste. We utilized the toilets as long as possible, flushing them with buckets of pond water that we used to refill the toilet tanks. However, the fact that the sewer lines weren't being flushed out by a sufficient volume of liquid soon caused a blockage, and we couldn't afford the health risks a backup of our sewage could create.

So, we dug latrines, one for the women and one for the men. We managed to make an effective "two-holer" for the ladies, using lumber and a couple of toilet seats. The men just straddled the trench military style, as had been done by soldiers for millennia. Tarps held up with stakes provided a visual barrier, but nothing could eliminate the smell. We had no quick lime to sprinkle over the excrement, and the clay soil didn't do the job, so we just had to keep filling them in and digging new ones inside the compound area for safety.

I remember stories about various Indian tribes on the Great Plains. Although they moved the village as they followed the herds of buffalo, they also sometimes were forced to move because they could no longer stand their own stench. We were in a similar situation. It's early April, and with the summer heat only a few weeks away, we must have a plan of action before that happens. A group meeting to discuss that will occur tomorrow, and I, as our unofficial leader, will preside. I'm not looking forward to it. Hard choices will have to be made. This is not going to be easy.

CHAPTER I

DECISIONS

It is what I feared, but also expected. The meeting was held, and I was elected to lead our exodus. My years of experience as an airline captain necessarily honed my leadership skills, but that was a long time ago, over seventeen years in the past. I suspect the real reason I was selected is that I own what may be the only functional motor vehicle left in Happy Valley, Old Red, my 1979 Jeep CJ-7. Like me, it's aged and worn, but it still functions.

Due to the fact that this forty-year-old vehicle didn't have a modern electronic ignition system, and what it did have was surrounded by enough steel to make an effective Faraday Cage, the EMP didn't render it useless as it did most other cars and trucks. It's only limiting factor is fuel and oil, and there is plenty of that in the gas tanks of the tens of thousands of abandoned cars on the streets and highways, or in deserted auto parts store shelves. We just have to syphon gas out of the cars, and take what motor oil we need from the mostly looted store shelves. Motor oil, now basically useless, wasn't on the looters shopping list.

The Jeep also has a trailer hitch, and when we find a suitable small trailer, we'll be able to use that to haul food, water and supplies, including ammunition, for the ordeal to come. We will all be armed. That is a given. As much as we'd like to believe that those we will encounter on our journey will be civilized and benevolent, the last years' experience has taught us otherwise. It will be us against the world until we finally find a place with enough natural resources to start over. None of us has any idea of how long it will take to get there, or where we will end up.

Since many of us have spent a lot of time in the western part of our state, we have decided to head up there, towards the Blue Ridge Mountains and a milder climate, at least for most of the year. Except for the population centers of Greenville and Spartanburg, Western South Carolina offers a place to grow food and hunt wild game for meat or catch fish in the numerous streams, rivers and lakes which abound in the area. Our daughter and her family live in Greer, a suburb of Greenville, and we are praying that like us, they have somehow managed to survive the debacle which has befallen our country, or perhaps the entire North American Continent for all we know.

Each member of our little band of survivors must be assigned specific tasks and responsibilities if we are to succeed. That process began as soon as our meeting broke up this afternoon. The first priority is self-defense, and the best marksmen among us must take on that task. I am among that group. We have become almost a tribe, equivalent to the Native American groups who populated our hemisphere for thousands of years after their ancestors came across the land bridge from Asia which existed during portions of the last Ice Age.

Those tribes constantly fought among themselves to protect their hunting grounds and other natural resources. It will probably be the same with us, but our age is surely our greatest enemy. We will have to link up with younger, stronger people if we are to survive until our inevitable end, and who knows when that date will be? Unless we plan and act wisely, it could be much sooner than we'd like.

The first task will be to find everything we will need on our coming trek, and that means leaving the safety of our compound to do so. The dangers of that mission concern me greatly. We'll start at first light in the morning, mindful of the threats which potentially lurk outside our small protected compound.

CHAPTER II

FORAGING

At first light the next day, four of us left the compound to start our foraging expedition. We have determined not to go farther than a one mile radius, and to be very careful. We don't want to be mistaken for looters. That could well be a death sentence if we happen upon another fortified compound such as ours. Because of our appearance we won't be confused with Eaters who generally attack alone anyway. The men of our group have kept their hair cut and shave daily, if only to maintain some sense of normality in the crazy world that now surrounds us. Some of the ladies still use makeup, but sparingly, to husband what little they have left.

A house to house search generally yields little useful material, the looters having swept most places clean months ago. However, we have become adept in discovering the hidden places where people secreted away treasured food substances, alcohol or ammunition, which is perhaps the most critical item on our list. With an ample supply of that, we can defend ourselves and hunt animals to provide critical protein. We are careful to also look for tobacco products. None of us has continued to smoke, but we all feel these items might be useful for bartering in the future. Baring a miracle restoration of civil order, money of any type has become worthless.

We can never be sure whether we will find a body, or even bodies in a dwelling we enter. The water in the p-traps under the sinks has long since evaporated, allowing the stench of the sewer lines to permeate an abandoned structure. We don't have running water in our compound, but we have been careful to keep our p-traps filled and use buckets to keep our toilets topped off as well, even though we no longer use them. We have taken to putting Vicks VapoRub under our noses before we enter a home, a practice long used by police or coroners when dealing with abandoned corpses.

As we entered the first dwelling on our list today, I had failed to spread the Vicks on my upper lip. The house was permeated with an unmistakable sickly-sweet odor. This was going to be a death house. When we entered the master bedroom, we found the source of the smell. Propped up on the headboard were the corpses of a man and woman. They had been dead for some time. Curiously, they were both in their nightclothes. He in a pair of pajamas and she in a frilly nightgown. The woman's head was leaning against the man's chest, and he had his left arm around her in what was obviously a final embrace. There was a bullet hole in her forehead. A matching hole was in his right temple, the weapon used was still clutched in his withered right hand, a small pistol, probably thirty-two caliber. They had both died instantly, but there were no horrific exit wounds, as would have been the case if a larger caliber weapon had been used. If we had seen them shortly after they died, they might have appeared to be asleep from a distance. These murder-suicides were not uncommon in retirement communities, even before the Event. For the last six months we had seen more, many more. Hunger, desperation and hopelessness were taking a grim toll.

Our search yielded little today. Happy Valley has apparently been pretty much cleaned out by looters or fellow compounders. We find an occasional bottle of antibiotics on the floor of a bathroom, discarded by looters who were looking for the pain killing drugs which are all too prevalent in senior citizen's medicine cabinets. It's obviously time to leave. First however, we need to do a complete inventory. Within reason, we must take everything useful with us, because we don't have any idea of how long it will take us to reach a safe haven in the western part of the state, if one is even available there.

One bright spot, we found a small trailer to tow behind my Jeep. It will triple our cargo carrying capacity. We also found a small foot powered air pump to keep the tires on the Jeep and trailer properly inflated. A small detail perhaps, but it is things like that which could make or break our chances for a successful journey.

CHAPTER III

INVENTORY

Prior to the suspected EMP attack, the only time most of us had to do an inventory was when we were making out a grocery list prior to a trip to the supermarket. What is required now is much more complex. We must also consider what can be reasonably carried by each individual.

Jack Swanson, a former high school history teacher, came up with a great idea. Why not make light weight, wheeled Indian style travois using tree saplings and bicycle wheels? He even came up with an idea for axles, using PVC electrical conduit salvaged from an abandoned building site. These contraptions should allow even the women in our group to carry up to one hundred pounds of supplies with relative ease. Necessity is indeed The Mother of Invention!

The heavy duty items, such as extra rifles or shotguns, ammunition, canned goods, water and gas cans will be carried in the Jeep or trailer, leaving the lighter stuff like clothing, medical supplies and sleeping bags for the travois or backpacks. One thing is mandatory. Each individual must be armed at all times, a rifle and handgun for the men and a handgun for the women. If we are the victims of an ambush, we must be able to respond immediately. Not to do this might be a fatal mistake.

We are pleasantly surprised at how much food we have for our journey. The canned goods are mostly gone, less than two hundred pounds remain. However, since there were many "preppers" in our neighborhood, we have over five hundred pounds of freeze-dried foods in mylar pouches. Since these are very light, they will provide thousands of nutritious meals for the group, especially since we have all become accustomed to eating smaller amounts daily. None of us is overweight. In fact, we are in the best shape we've enjoyed for years. Several former diabetics no longer require insulin shots, diet has reduced their blood sugar levels to pre-diabetic levels. The same for high blood pressure, ulcers and hip or knee pains. We're at our optimum weight or below, and our bodies are rewarded because of that fact.

One issue has now come to the forefront. It is simply what we must leave behind. I am reminded of the tales of visitors to portions of the Santa Fe Trail. It was easy to find, because of the deep ruts in the sandstone made by the iron rimmed wheels of the Conestoga covered wagons used by most of the early westward bound pioneers. Alongside those ruts were the sad remnants of furniture and other heavy belongings which had to be discarded when it became evident that not to do so would overtax the pulling capacity of the oxen team. All too frequently there were crudely fashioned crosses or other grave markers, showing the last resting places of family members who must also be left behind. It is a sobering thought that the same might happen to some of us on our own trek to the West.

So, family photo albums must be culled to only a very few important mementos. Those of us who saved a lot of pictures on our computer hard drives are out of luck unless we saved backup copies on flash drives or DVDs, which might become useful in the future if we can once again access working computers. Large family bibles must be left, but small versions of the New Testament will probably be part of the load for some of us, I'm sure.

One of our more ardent preppers had made it a habit to keep his laptop computer, a cellphone and a handheld GPS in a Faraday Cage of his own devising. It was simply a Homer Bucket from the Home Depot, with a plastic lid and lined with many layers of aluminum foil which was then placed in a metal garbage can, with a metal lid. He had started doing this after reading a report detailing the threat of a possible EMP attack on our country which was published in 2008, but largely ignored by the media and politicians. Part of that report estimated that up to ninety percent of the population of our country could be dead within a year after such a catastrophe. Had this come true? We weren't sure, but it was more and more likely to be the case. Unfortunately, the batteries on his electronics had long since been depleted. Perhaps we could figure out a way to recharge them using the Jeeps alternator, but that would have to wait until we felt once again safe in our new location.

Clothing was something else. In the Low Country of South Carolina, winters are very mild, temperatures rarely dropping below freezing. Upstate, particularly in the mountainous areas, it would be another matter. So those who had rain repellant winter garments must take them. Gloves as well, if we had any. Several pairs of substantial shoes were a must, lightweight walking type preferred. My wife Dottie and I also had Maine style Duck Boots, which although heavier, were warm and waterproof. We were definitely bringing them, along with the heavy duty socks they required.

A week's worth of underwear and socks, four pair of hiking shorts and four pairs of durable long pants like blue jeans are the best choice for men and women. Finally, four cotton blend golf shirts and two long sleeved shirts, plus one medium weight sweater filled out the wardrobe, with several hats of course, golf and wide brimmed preferred. That should last at least another year, with careful washing and maintenance. Medicine and medical supplies were by mutual consent pooled when we formed our defensive compound. We are blessed that two of our group, Janet Lewis and Peggy Fleming, are retired Registered Nurses, and one was a surgical scrub nurse who assisted in many serious surgeries. Janet has the knowledge and skill to sew up open wounds and even set broken bones, tasks we hope she won't have to perform, but could if needed. Peg worked at a large metropolitan hospital in the emergency room. She has seen and treated everything from heart attack cases to gunshot wounds and everything in between. As I said, we are very fortunate to have their skills available to us on our journey.

Janet and Peggy have done a complete inventory of the medicines and medical supplies we have collected. They assure me that we have a more than adequate amount of pain killers and antibiotics to sustain a group like ours for an extended period of time, certainly more than a year. Bandages and first aid supplies are also more than adequate for our future needs as well.

Next, come the last three items, the barter stuff, liquor and cigarettes, and the all-important ammunition and water. As I said, we no longer smoke, so the cigarettes are solely for bartering purposes. The liquor has a dual use, for barter, or to be used as a disinfectant for open wounds. The ammunition is priceless. It is our provider when we hunt, and our defender should the need arise. We will always carry several five-gallon cans of water to fill our canteens, but we have many ways to filter water to make it safe to drink, including Life Straws, which can be used to drink directly from almost any source of fresh water.

Although we will avoid all confrontations, it would be foolish on our part not to realize that they will probably occur in the future, and our age works against us. Our gray and white hair marks us as senior citizens, and as such, easy prey in some people's minds. To limit that as much as possible, another product goes on our list of necessities, hair dye. We have agreed that we'll all use it before we leave, and during our journey. From a distance at least, we will appear years younger, and as such less vulnerable to attack.

CHAPTER IV

THE CACHE

As we did our inventory, one thing became very clear to all of us. The crisis we faced made us decide to leave not just things, but indeed vital parts of our family history, as we began the trek westward. Photo albums, treasured artwork, family heirlooms like silverware and jewelry must be left behind if we are to survive. It was gut wrenching. But then Jack Swanson again came to our rescue.

One day, when we were discussing the problem, Jack said "Why don't we build a cache?" Being a bit of a history buff myself, I realized that he was referring to the practice used by early nineteenth century mountain men and fur traders to bury vital items like gun powder, lead for shot, extra traps and bound beaver pelts, for retrieval later, should something occur which made their transport back to civilization impossible at the time. The loss of pack horses or mules to raiding parties of Indians was a common occurrence, and made the practice of "caching" frequently a necessity.

So, after we discussed the concept with the group, we determined to dig our own cache, to bury and hopefully protect the items we had to leave behind, but in the hope that we, or family members, could come back and retrieve these personal treasures if sanity and order returned to our existence in the future.

Because of the high water table in Happy Valley we couldn't make the pit too deep. Two feet was the maximum. So, we determined to make it two feet deep, four feet wide and twenty feet long. It took a week of hard labor to excavate. Thankfully we had no rain during that period or the following three days required to place the items and cover the cache.

Each family had roughly ten cubic feet of cache to use. We placed the items in plastic tubs with lids, and sealed them all with candle wax and duct tape. Silver, jewelry, and photos, along with paintings and lithographs which had been removed from their frames and carefully rolled, were our treasures. The bottom and sides of the cache were lined with overlapping hurricane shutters, the plastic tubs were sealed in plastic sheets secured with more duct tape, and then everything was covered with more shutters and dirt. Finally, the sod we had carefully removed was placed on top. Within a few days, you would not know the cache existed.

As a final precaution, we took all the remaining dirt from the pit and threw it into the woods several lots down from our compound. A last task was to make hand-written copies of the location of the cache in relation to the foundation of our house, even if it was destroyed by fire. Our personal family history and treasures were now as secure as we could make them.

All this might seem to be a waste of time, but indeed that was one item we had in abundance. The last year had shaken us to our very core. The loss of friends to violent attacks, disease, and depression induced suicides, plus the nagging fear that the same might have occurred to the members of our own families, was becoming almost too much to bear. None of us were young. We all had our share of the aches and pains that come with advancing years. However, those of us who had survived thus far all had an intense desire to live a little longer, if only to find out what had actually caused this awful tragedy, and for Dottie and I to discover whether my daughter Megan, her husband Matt and our grandchildren, were still alive and well.

The building of the cache and the preservation of some of the elements of our lives together was symbolic of a mutual desire to leave something of us protected and behind, for us or members of our family to someday be able to return and retrieve. I just hoped that it wasn't in fact a kind of time capsule, to be someday discovered by humans or other beings in the distant future, and pondered over as we have looked at similar deposits made by other people thousands of years in the past.

CHAPTER V

DEPARTURE DAY - ADIOS!

We have no idea how far we will be able to walk each day. Obviously, we have to toughen up our bodies after over a year of very little physical activity due to the fact we have been mostly restricted to remaining in our defensive compound. Of greatest concern is our feet. Although we all have good quality walking shoes, we're not looking at a few miles of travel, we're looking at over two hundred and twenty miles, much of it uphill, just to reach the vicinity of Greer, South Carolina, where our daughter, son-in-law and granddaughters live.

We will start slowly. My plan is to have us walk at a reasonable pace for two hours and then rest for half an hour. We will be maintaining the pace of our slowest member, as it is vital to stay close together for safety. I hope to walk at least ten miles per day, so it will take us between two to three weeks just to reach Greer, and that depends on not being impeded in any way. By my calculations we will pass through eighteen towns on the way to Greer, several of them with pre-event populations of over five thousand people. Ten miles will just get us to the vicinity of I-95, but the way should be clear, walking down a four-lane paved road with good visibility all the way. I don't want to dwell on the possibility of an attack on our little group, but it is always in the back of my mind. The first two days will be through areas which were fairly densely populated prior to the mysterious "Event". I will feel safer when we reach more rural areas.

Several of our group are history buffs, and we have decided to apply techniques used by the Roman Legions and Boer Trekkers when they were on the move through possibly hostile country. At the end of each days march the legionnaires would dig a palisaded ditch around the camp to defend against attack. We of course can't do that but will "laager" the wagons so to speak, as the Boers did on their "trek" into the South African interior. We will use the Jeep and trailer, as well as the wheeled travois, to surround our campsite. We'll build small fires around the perimeter for defensive illumination, with our cooking fire in the center of the laager. Armed guards will be posted at all four points of the compass, so we'll have to sleep in rotation. I believe it is vital to maintain this defensive mindset. Growing complacent could quickly prove fatal. Again, we just don't know what's out there. Even packs of roaming feral dogs could become a serious threat. The other factor we must always consider is having our camps in open spaces, with no trees or buildings nearby which could conceal the approach of a potential predator, human or animal. So, at seven o'clock in the morning on April twenty-first, we began our trek into the unknown. I wish we could have taken pictures of the group, but no one has a functioning camera or phone, a reality of our "Brave New World". It's about a mile walk to the front entrance of the community. We are astounded at the sights we witness. All the previously manicured lawns are overgrown with weeds, and untrimmed shrubs nearly hide some of the smaller homes, where only the roofs are visible. The ponds are choked with grasses and debris. Here and there stands the gutted shell of a house. We knew there had been some fires, but couldn't imagine there were so many. Chaos has indeed reigned over our community.

The other factor we all were aware of was an almost total lack of sound. With the exception of the wind through the trees, nothing could be heard. No barking dogs, no crows or other noisy birds, and of course no sounds of human activity, just an eerie silence. Fallen trees are everywhere, some neatly cut down with a saw, others crudely felled with an axe. Firewood? Poles for barricades? We don't know, but it could be either. Along Happy Valley Boulevard we don't see any indication of barricaded enclaves like ours, just devastation and neglect.

We reached the entrance in just over half an hour. I was concerned that we might be pushing it a bit, but we continued on for the full two hours, turning westbound on US-278 towards Hardeeville, where we would presumably stop for the day. Don Davis, the last one out, turned around and saluted. "Adios Happy Valley" he said.

Since the suspected EMP attack had probably occurred in the middle of the night, there were few deserted cars on the highway. We only encountered two in the first hour of our hike. We stopped for our initial rest period just past the numerous car dealerships that lined that part of US-278. The lots were full of cars and trucks which apparently hadn't been vandalized. They were filthy of course, but not damaged, having become useless pieces of metal after all their computer chips had been fried by the suspected EMP. The Wal-Mart, CVS Pharmacy and Publix Supermarket had obviously been looted of anything of value, with broken windows and doors ripped off their hinges. There were no signs of people, however, just the same eerie silence.

Janet and Peggy, our official Medics, spent part of the rest period checking people's feet for signs of blistering. This could quickly render an otherwise healthy individual into a helpless cripple, and that must be avoided at all costs. Thankfully, none were noted, but then we had only covered two miles of the desired ten for the day. Time to start again. We found our first body about a mile down the road. Just scattered bones really, but the skull showed signs of a heavy blow to the head by a blunt object, maybe a bat or a hammer. Peggy called it a depressed skull fracture, and she figured the person died instantly. Who did it or when is unknown, but it could have been relatively recently, since the vultures and insects clean all the flesh off the bone and devour the internal organs in a remarkably short period of time in this climate. Could the killer still be in the vicinity? These were definitely bad vibes for our first night on the road. We finally made camp that night in an open field about a mile west of I-95, a distance of roughly twelve miles from our compound. A good start, but can we keep up the pace?

CHAPTER VI

IS THAT GUNFIRE?

We had a bad night. We all suffered from insect bites. Unfortunately, insect repellant was one of the things which we had neglected to stockpile, and a wet winter has made the low country swamps a perfect breeding ground for mosquitos and biting gnats. The sooner we get to higher, drier ground the better, but until that time we will just have to endure the swarms.

The second day found us anything but rested. Sore feet and leg cramps interrupted what little deep sleep we had at our first laager. Sometime during the night, a tree fell in the forest next to our field, and all of us were instantly awake, many with weapons at the ready. We must stop this and learn to trust our sentries. Without sufficient rest each night we won't be able to continue to keep up our walking pace every day. During the last year in our compound, we slept in our own bed. Now, due to the lack of air mattresses, we are sleeping on the hard ground, without even the comfort of a pillow. That was a mistake, albeit a small one. I remembered the technique of digging a small depression for my shoulder and hip from my youth as a Boy Scout. I did the same for my wife Dottie and will teach it to the others when we make camp tonight.

I have always kept maps in our car, even though for the last ten years or more we have had a built in GPS. Those devices are useless now, and with the flat terrain of the South Carolina Low Country we can't follow visual landmarks as we often did in the mountainous west, where I spent most of my life. Incredibly, none of us owned a simple compass, so if we can't follow the sun to Greer, we'll have to follow highways. I plotted as straight a route as possible on my AAA South Carolina roadmap, and we will follow that.

The only downside of following highways is that it will constantly take us through small towns along the way, and we can't count on any surviving residents being friendly to a tribe of outsiders passing through their territory. All we can realistically do is hope for the best, but expect the worst.

As the sun set on the second day of our trek, we prepared to set up our laager in a plowed field a reasonable distance from a small wooded area and next to a single farmhouse and small barn. A thunderstorm was brewing just west of us, and there was intermittent lightning and thunder from that. Suddenly, we heard three loud pops which were definitely not sounds of nature. We all looked at each other. Is that gunfire, and if so, which direction did it come from? Needless to say, that was not conducive to a restful night's sleep.

However, lighting our fires and posting our sentries, we all bedded down for the night.

The next morning, we enjoyed a special treat, a cup of brewed coffee. That sort of shows how our lives have changed in the last year. A mundane occurrence which basically happened every morning of our lives in the past has now somehow become special. I am beginning to realize that we had become prisoners and jailers alike in our Happy Valley compound, waiting for a reprieve or pardon which was just not forthcoming. For better or worse, we will have to provide that for ourselves.

We were on the road by seven thirty. I know that because I have one of the few working watches in the group. My Citizen Eco-Drive wristwatch derives its power from sunlight, so a battery doesn't have to be replaced on a regular basis. A few of the women have old fashioned spring wound watches as well. I have to fight off the vague feeling of guilt that I am the only one who is not walking, dragging a wheeled travois behind me. I hope the others understand that I am the only one who understands the mechanical condition of the Jeep, with its slipping clutch and leaking rear seal that I never got around to repairing before what we now refer to as "The Event". If the Jeep fails, we have lost an essential survival tool, and as our elected leader, I can't allow that to happen.

We have decided that it is necessary for us to have scouts, who walk ahead of us to warn the group if they spot any potential trouble. This advice came from Dave Carson, who was an Army Ranger during the Vietnam War. He has volunteered to be our permanent point man and will select others to check our flanks on a rotational basis. All are of course fully armed with AR-15s and handguns. The only caveat is that our point man and flankers must always remain in sight of the caravan.

We walk through the day, keeping to our schedule of two hours walking followed by half hour rest periods. We always take a full hour lunch break, during which time many of us enjoy a short nap. This seems to be working well so far on fairly flat terrain. We may have to adjust it when we begin the gradual ascent into the South Carolina Piedmont and the High Country.

Around four o'clock in the afternoon, Carson suddenly paused and raised a hand in the universal signal to halt. He is looking towards a tall stand of trees about three quarters of a mile in front of him and gets out his binoculars for a closer look. He immediately drops to one knee, and waves his arm palm down indicating we should all do likewise, but what has he seen? I unconsciously reach for my sidearm, not to unholster it, but to reassure me it's there. I suspect others are doing the same thing. Is danger ahead? We are completely in the open, walking down a two-lane road with no real cover, except shallow roadside ditches, until we reach the tree line.

Dave drops back, running in a crouched manner. He is obvious concerned, but about what? We surround him and wait for an answer as soon as he can catch his breath. "Tree-houses" he finally says. "A bunch of them". "I saw a brief flash of light. I'm guessing it was a reflection from a rifle scope or binoculars. We're being watched".

CHAPTER VII

THE TREE PEOPLE

After much discussion, I decide to form our laager and wait until morning to investigate. We don't know who is up in the trees, or why they have chosen to build these structures. It must be a form of defense, but from whom or what? We can't take a chance that our sudden appearance will be determined to be a threat, but we can't realistically avoid the area either. With our wheeled travois, cross country travel is nearly impossible. We must continue up the road, which runs directly through the woods containing the treehouses. To do this we must have the permission of the people up in the trees. How to obtain this will be a matter of much discussion as soon as our nightly laager is established.

After considerable debate, we decide to send a single member up the road under a flag of truce. We want to do everything we can to ensure our emissaries' safety. Dave Carson was one of the more ardent preppers in our community. One of the things he purchased was a bullet-proof vest similar to those worn by the military and law enforcement. Because of his position as our point man he wears it daily. He knows that it isn't really bullet-proof, but sort of bullet resistant, depending on the caliber of the weapon. Dave has volunteered to attempt to make contact with what we now refer to as the Tree People, and try to negotiate a safe passage through their territory. He knows it will be dangerous, but that we basically have no choice.

In the morning we decide to move our caravan to a point just out of rifle range for anything but a trained sniper with a high caliber sniper rife. This will allow the people in the tree house village to see the size and composition of our group. The downside of this action is it makes it obvious to them that we are all armed, and as such potentially dangerous. It will be up to Dave to convince them that we mean no harm but are just passing through on our way west. Will they listen and agree? We can only hope so.

We move forward as planned, and then Dave slowly advances to within a hundred feet of the edge of the woods. He is carrying a stick with a pair of panties tied to the end. That is the only item of white cloth we could find. Dave stops, and makes a deliberate show of disarming himself, slowly placing his AR-15 on the ground, followed by his sidearm. He turns in a circle with his hands in the air, so the observers in the treehouses can see he is unarmed. Then he walks forward, panty stick in hand, until he can converse with the Tree People. We all hold our breath. His head is tilted up, and he is obviously having a conversation, but we can hear nothing due to the distance. After about five minutes, he turns around, walks back, picks up his weapons, and returns to our anxiously waiting group. We are shocked to hear what he has to say.

"Boars" he says. "They're up there because of wild boars". The treehouse dwellers initially built the structures after they had been attacked by roving bands of looters in the first months following the Event, when it became obvious that there was no law enforcement to prevent looters from preying on people weaker than themselves. Those attacks finally stopped, as the looters moved on to greener pastures for their looting activities, but then an even more deadly menace arose.

Wild boars had populated the area for years and were a popular game choice for hunters from South Carolina and the surrounding states. These ferocious creatures mated with feral domestic hogs which had escaped from their pens, and created a super variety of very large and aggressive animals who had no fear of humans in the least. Their cruel tusks could inflict horrible wounds, and were even capable of disemboweling an unwary victim, which apparently had been the awful fate of several local residents. The Tree People were poorly armed, and didn't venture out of the treehouses except to forage for food or hunt small game and deer for meat. Those hunting trips were fraught with danger, and not done until hunger made them necessary.

We were given permission to pass through their territory, and did so as quickly as possible, due to the stench of human excrement deposited on the forest floor from the outhouses in the treetops. The tree people must pray for another winter to kill the smell. They can't move, so they must endure it in hotter weather.

CHAPTER VIII

THE BOAR

We bypassed the town of Estill and put another twelve miles behind us today, constantly on the lookout for the wild boars which had made an entire community into a real version of the fictional Swiss Family Robinsons. We were especially vigilant in the vicinity of heavily forested areas, which are prevalent in this part of the state. The road we travel is frequently bordered by live oaks, whose Spanish Moss draped branches often form a natural tunnel, blocking out most of the sunlight. We enjoyed driving through these in the past, but now they are cause for concern. Do they harbor and conceal deadly predators, just waiting to attack?

In the late afternoon we came to a bridge over a fast-moving small river with crystal clear water flowing over a sandy bottom. It has now been nearly a week since any of us has bathed, and the opportunity to do so is irresistible. Dave has informed us that a good spot for our nightly laager is just ahead in a large hayfield. So, segregated by sex, we decide it's time to take a bath and then wash some clothing as well.

The women go first, with the men, backs turned to protect the ladies' modesty, stand on the crest of the hill bordering the South side of the river. Soon the air is filled with the shouts and giggles of our wives, first complaining that the water is too cold, and then just enjoying the experience of getting clean, au natural.

Suddenly, the air was filled with a horrible shriek, followed by the frantic cries of our women. We all ran towards the riverbank to see what has happened and behold a sight which is both terrifying and funny at the same time. Six of the ladies are standing naked in the middle of the river while the remaining four, all now screaming at the top of their lungs, are six to eight feet up in the pine trees which line the other bank. At the base of the trees stands an enormous boar, a thousand pounds at least, with his head raised, showing the murderous razor-sharp curved tusks which must be at least six inches in length. He occasionally butts a tree, making its occupant scream all the louder. All we can see from our bank is four female backsides, but note that Charlene Davis, our Southern Belle from an old Georgia family, is one of the treed victims, as even from a distance we can see that she is wearing her ever present pearls.

We must do something, and quick, because the boar might soon dislodge one of the tree climbers. However, the distance is over two hundred feet, and a miss-aimed shot or ricochet could injure or kill one of the four. I don't have my scope mounted AR-15. It's back in the Jeep, and I'm not confident of the abilities of those of us who are armed with rifles.

Suddenly, three shots ring out from the other side of the river and the boar falls over, mortally wounded or dead. A man in camouflage clothing steps from behind a tree about two hundred yards to our right on the far side of the river. He is carrying a scope mounted rifle.

As I studied this individual, I heard someone walk up behind me and felt a hand on my shoulder. I turned to see Ari Zuckerman. "What's up Rabbi?" I said. "Let me come with you." He said. Ari is indeed an ordained Jewish Rabbi, but he also is a former officer in the Israel Defense Forces and has fought in several of the wars against neighboring Arab states that Israel has had to endure since its inception in 1948. He has become sort of a non-denominational spiritual advisor to our group since the Event prevented him and his wife Rachael from returning to Israel, where they lived for half of each year since they purchased their home in Happy Valley. He is kind, but behind that peaceful exterior, I believe he has a soul of iron, a good man to be at your back in an emergency.

"Sure" I said. "Glad to have you. Let's go".

CHAPTER IX

THE DEER HUNTER

We crossed the bridge over the river and turned left to introduce ourselves to the savior of our four ladies in distress. As
we got closer, we realized that he was quite young, perhaps in
his early to mid-twenties. He wasn't in an aggressive posture at
all, with his rifle on a sling behind his back. I saw no sidearm.

"Al Farragut" I said, extending my hand. "What can I
say but thanks, that boar was a monster!" "Bill Mason" he
replied. "Yeah, those bastards are meaner than shit, and you
can't outrun 'em".

"This is Rabbi Zuckerman" I said. "Just Ari will do" said
Ari, extending his hand. "My thanks as well". "Great shooting
by the way! Two to the chest and one to the head I believe".

By this time the husbands of the four tree climbers had
crossed the river with towels and clothing. They formed a
ring, facing outward, so the women could dry off and regain

their dignity. When that was accomplished, we all walked over to examine the dead boar.

"I've seen bigger, but not many" said Bill. "We'll get at least six hundred pounds of good meat off of that one if you'll help me field dress and cut it up". "I can smoke some, and make jerky and pemmican out of the rest. After our pig roast, that is". "I guess you won't be able to join us for that Rabbi".

"Says who?" Said Ari. "Haven't you ever heard of Israeli white steak?" "Anyway, under our present circumstances, I'm sure I could get a dispensation from our Chief Rabbi, like Catholics used to receive from a Bishop if they had to eat meat as part of an airline meal on Fridays, before that custom was abandoned by the church".

I turned to Bill and said "Are you living out here alone, or as part of a group?" "It's just me and my wife Suzi since her father died of a heart attack a couple of months back" "We never leave the farm. We've got everything we need out here, and bad things were happening in town after all the electronic stuff quit last year." "People went kind of crazy".

"But we do have a problem now. Suzi was taking birth control pills after were married three years ago, but those ran out, and she just told me she thinks she's pregnant. Guess she has missed a couple of periods". "She's terrified of having to deliver our baby with no doctor around, only me to help her. What if something goes wrong?"

Without hesitation I said, "Well we have two Registered Nurses in our group who would be glad to help her". "We can't stay here though, but you're welcome to join us if you'd like. We're headed west to find our family if they're still there.

They live in the Greenville/Spartanburg area." "How far is your farm from here?"

"It's only a couple of miles, and I have to get home before dark or Suzi will worry". "Let's field dress and butcher this boar. I've got salt to help preserve the meat until we can smoke it for jerky and roast up the rest tomorrow. I'll go home for the night. Will you camp around here?"

"Yes". I said. "In the open field just up the road". "We laager our travois and have armed guards in shifts all night, so don't come back until full light in the morning."

Bill didn't understand the words laager or travois. When I explained the concept, he said "Wow, you guys are really careful. Have you run into any trouble?" "Not on the road so far," I said "But last year in Happy Valley was a nightmare. That's one of the reasons we left."

As we worked on the boar, Bill explained that although they had a milk cow and chickens on the farm, he and Suzi had a craving for red meat, so he would occasionally stalk and kill a deer for extra protein. He said he always came in this direction, so the sound of his gunfire wouldn't be heard in the town, and attract unwanted attention, including potential looters.

As the sun set in the late afternoon sky, Bill left for home, promising to return in the morning and bring Suzi with him. As he walked across the field, I had the feeling that he and Suzi could be valuable assets to the group. We needed some young blood added to our caravan, and his skills as hunter, outdoorsman and farmer would surely come in handy in the future.

We set up our nightly laager in the open field where we told Bill he could find us in the morning. As an added precaution, we distributed pieces of the boar's internal organs and intestines around the outside of the laager to hopefully discourage an attack by another wild boar in the vicinity. It had been a long and eventful day.

When they arrived in the morning, they were both riding horses. We were all a bit taken aback. None of us had seen a horse for over a year, and only a few had actually ridden one. Bill was on a gray stallion and Suzi rode a beautiful pure white mare. He later explained that it had been his plan to start breeding the pair, and slowly transform Suzi's family farm into a working horse ranch.

The Event put a halt to all that. Veterinarians are desirable for a successful foaling, and none were now available. They had been careful to corral the mare from the stallion when she was in heat. Their plans, like many others, had been put on hold.

Suzi was a delight. She wasn't yet showing signs of her pregnancy, but she already exhibited the glow which all pregnant ladies seem to have. We introduced her to Janet and Peggy, our two R/N designated Medics. They immediately hit it off, and I could almost see Suzi give a sigh of relief. She would be protected when the baby came.

We decided to take the boar carcass to the farm to have our pig roast and smoke the jerky. We loaded the meat on the trailer and followed Bill and Suzi to the farm. It took about three quarters of an hour over a series of country roads, the last one a dirt track about half a mile long. The farm is in a small valley, and out of sight of any roads. Perhaps that's why it was not pillaged by looters from the town.

There are only two bedrooms, so we happily had a lottery to determine who would be the Guests of the House, and sleep in a real bed. The Swanson's won, and we were all happy for them. Bill and Suzi opened her father's liquor cabinet, and offered the contents to our group for a drink before our pig roast feast the next afternoon. Suzi's father had built a full-size smoker, which Bill used to smoke our boar meat feast. It took 20 hours to prepare the meat, and the result was spectacular. In Italy, they refer to wild boar as Cinghiale, and it is regarded as a great delicacy. We all enjoyed our best meal in recent memory, with fresh corn on the cob and potatoes grown on the farm. We also were treated to eggs. Eggs in profusion. None of us has enjoyed an egg for over a year. We must find a way to bring the hens and a rooster with us when we depart.

The next few days were spent smoking and drying the boar jerky on racks that Suzi's father built years ago. We also harvested all the corn and potatoes we could possibly carry. A wonderful and tasty supplement to our freeze-dried foods. Too soon it was time to leave and resume our trek. An added bonus is an ancient wagon from the farm. It is perfectly serviceable, and will be pulled by the horses. It almost doubles our cargo carrying capacity. We would leave the next morning, rested and ready for what is ahead. The next few days would prove that we are a bit naive in our expectations of a safe and uneventful passage. We would soon be disabused of that notion.

CHAPTER X

AMBUSH!

We left the farm early the next morning. It is always easier to make good time while it's relatively cool. Our goal was to get as close to Allendale as we could that day. We wanted to set up our laager early that afternoon, and planned to quickly transit the area at first light in the morning. Bill told us that he thought that inmates from the Allendale Correctional Institute were among the looters who ravaged the local area in the months after the Event.

We developed a plan of action that would allow us to have everyone ride on the Jeep, trailer or wagon, piling the travois and their contents on top and trailing a couple behind the trailer and wagon. Using this method, we should be able to make better time, perhaps as much as five miles per hour, until we were well past the possible danger that Allendale presented.

The laager was set up as planned, and we made the illumination fires around the perimeter larger than normal, so we could see any possible attackers from a greater distance. That concept turned out to be a near fatal mistake, because the fires exposed us as well. We had a meal of freeze-dried vegetables and boar jerky, and bedded down as soon as it became dark. All went well until shortly after midnight, when Dan Lewis, one of the designated sentries, suddenly cried out in pain. I was immediately wide awake, and heard another person cry out as well. I looked over to where Dan had been standing and was astounded to see him lying on his back clutching the shaft of an arrow which was protruding from his left shoulder. A few yards to the left I saw Pat McCartie grimacing in pain as she too held onto an arrow which had struck her mid-thigh on her left leg. The soft "thump" of additional arrows meant we were still under attack from an unknown enemy outside the illuminated circle around our laager. "Under the Jeep, trailer and wagon!" I shouted. "Take cover!" "Quickly!"

Ari acted with the skill of a trained combat fighter. Since it was impossible to determine where the arrows were coming from, he methodically began firing shots from his AR-15, moving slowly in a circle. Dave Carson followed his lead, and back to back they gradually covered the entire 360-degree space around the laager. I heard a scream from the darkness, and the barrage of arrows suddenly stopped.

We pulled Dan and Pat under the wagon to tend to their injuries, and I was glad to see that the entry wound was only as big as the arrow shaft. They were obviously target arrows, with a small metal point, not hunting arrows, with razor sharp four bladed tips. A quick pull and the shafts were removed by former E/R nurse Peggy Fleming. "And I thought I'd seen it all" she said, shaking her head. She quickly cleaned and dressed the wounds with the assistance of our other R/N medic Janet Lewis, wife of Dan. They assured us that the injuries were thankfully not serious, and would heal after a week or so with the use of antibiotic ointment and clean dressings daily.

We spent the rest of the night hunkered down under the cover of the Jeep, trailer and wagon. At first light we discovered that one of the horses, the stallion, had also been hit. An arrow was protruding from his left flank. It too proved to be superficial, and Peggy tended to him as well. Considering the circumstances, we had been extremely lucky. It could have been worse, much worse.

Fully armed and alert, we walked outside the perimeter of our laager to try to find clues as to who had attacked us. About a hundred feet out we discovered a blood trail, which led to the edge of a wooded area. There, we found the body of a middle-aged man. He had been gut shot and crawled this far before he died from loss of blood. He was probably the one who cried out in the dark last night, and had obviously been one of the archers. We all agreed that he had not acted alone, but what were we going to do about the ambush?

When we turned the body over to check for other weapons or identification, stenciled on the back of his jacket was "South Carolina Department of Corrections". Did this mean he was a SCDC officer, or an escaped inmate? We didn't know for sure, since there was nothing on the body to identify him. His body was in full rigor mortis. We pondered if we should give him the courtesy of a burial, but decided it wasn't worth our effort. After all, he had tried to murder us in our sleep. So, we left him to the mercies of scavengers, it was all he deserved.

I called what could only be termed a War Council, and all attended, including our two wounded members. "We've got to go through Allendale" I said. "There's no practical way to get around it". "We have been attacked by an unknown number of people who were willing to kill us all to get what we have". "We can't allow them another bite at that apple. We're going to have to appear strong, not weak, and if that means shooting, and even killing someone to make the point, we will have to do it!"

That statement brought a stunned silence from the group. We had previously only acted in self-defense, when threatened by a mentally deranged Eater, and only Dave Carson and I had actually killed one. Would the others have the guts to take a life if the need arose? Right now, they were Warriors in name only.

The silence was broken by Ari Zuckerman. "Al's right". He said. "Both Rachael and I have family members who died in the Holocaust, and I have fought in two very bitter wars to defend myself and my country from people who I didn't hate. It's the other way around, they hated ME, and just because I come from another tribe of the same Semitic group that bears our DNA roots as well but chose to worship in another way. It's crazy, but I had no other choice than kill or be killed."

"We are now in the same boat." He continued. "Now, it's not about religion, it's about food, and water, and all the other things required to survive". "We can't possibly befriend everyone we meet along the way like we did Bill and Suzi." "Bill's actions defended US, and probably saved the life of at least one of our party." "His skills, and those of Suzi's, her being a farm raised girl, will benefit us all in the future." "Our contribution is to provide medical help with her pregnancy, and strength in numbers for mutual self-defense". "It may have been kind to take them in, but it also made sense. We have to look at that concept every time it comes up in the future, as it surely will".

He slowly turned his head to survey the group, and I noticed that he had put on his yarmulke, which he didn't wear every day, but always when giving religious council. "We are going to do some things that we would normally never do, if we are to survive in the future." "We will probably have to injure or kill people as well." "However, we will never do it unless it is absolutely necessary, and we will not do it to gain something which is not ours." "We are not like the Nazis, and never will be." "So enough discussion, let's leave this thing to nature." He said, gesturing at the body. "And get moving".

We placed Pat McCartie and Dan Lewis in the back of the Jeep, surrounded by boxed food items, for some protection from arrows or bullets if we were attacked again. With Dave Carson once more in the lead, we headed for Allendale. What we would find when we got there was anyone's guess, but I felt that Ari's speech had got the group in the right frame of mind to do whatever needed to be done. The Water Lily Warriors were about to go on the offensive, and they were pissed!

CHAPTER XI

REPRISAL

As it turned out, we were much closer to the Allendale Correctional Institution than we thought. Less than two miles up the road, it came into view on the left-hand side. It was apparently deserted, and we noticed that all the gates through the high, razor wire topped chain link fence were open. Not a soul was in sight. Dave once again raised his arm in a STOP gesture. We complied, and he took out his binoculars and carefully surveyed the facility.

After a few minutes, he walked back to the Jeep. "It looks clear, but I still think we should be very wary of this place and get past it as quickly as possible." He said. I agreed. There had been many armed guards who were watching over some really bad people in this place. It might not be a maximum-security prison, but the bulk of the inmates weren't choirboys either. The question was, where did everybody go? Did all the locks open automatically after the total power failure, or was there a backup system which kept everything under control until it ran out of fuel? We had no way of knowing. All we knew was that the inmates could still be around, or possibly not. I hoped for a mass exodus.

Another several miles and we were in Allendale proper. Again, no signs of life until a shot kicked up the dust a couple of feet in front of Dave. "Who the hell are you?" A loud voice exclaimed. "Don't come any closer!" "We're just passing through." Dave said. "We don't mean you any harm." "We'll decide if you pass through our town." The voice continued. "What you got in the wagon and trailer?" "None of your business." Said Dave. "Let us go in peace." The answer to that came quickly. Another shot, and Dave fell over, clutching his upper left chest. We were all shocked to see him fall, but were relieved to see him roll to his right and hide behind a concrete planter on the sidewalk next to him. "I'm okay, I'm okay!" He said. "Smoke the bastards!"

We immediately recovered from our shock and put down a concentrated fire on the spot where the hostile shots had come from, directed by Ari. "We've got to flank those bastards!" He said. "Come with me!" Without hesitation, I followed, crouching low and continuing to fire my AR-15 in the general direction where the hostile fire had come from. Dave was now back in action behind his cover. He kept up a continuous covering fire which kept our adversaries' heads down, and allowed Ari and I to move forward in relative safety. After a few feet, we were behind some trees, and looking straight down a line of men who were hiding behind a low brick wall and occasionally firing at Dave and the rest of the caravan. I looked at Ari and he just nodded.

We both rose up and began firing at the group. They didn't know we were there, and were taken completely by surprise. Six of them fell to the ground, and the rest fled in panic.

In retrospect, it all seemed to have happened in slow motion. I guess that's how the human mind works when confronted with an almost incomprehensible situation. Ari and I slowly rose from our position and motioned the others to come up. When they got there, we were witnesses to an awful sight. Six bodies, all on the ground, their weapons in their lifeless hands. We had killed them all. "Enough!" "Snap out of it" shouted Ari. "We've got to get moving!" "NOW!"

We moved off, almost in a daze, but were not confronted further as we left Allendale. We were no longer considered potential prey, but had been converted to predators, dangerous, and to be avoided at all costs. I hoped that reputation would precede us in the future. Our safety depended on it. Next on the route was Barnwell, which had a fairly large regional airport. I was eager to get there. I had a plan growing in my brain. We needed airborne reconnaissance, and maybe I could give it to us. We spent an anxious night in our laager just short of the Barnwell airport, but without incident. Apparently, our forceful retribution against our attackers had paid off. We weren't being followed.

CHAPTER XII

FLYBOY

One of the tools I had brought from my workbench was a large pair of bolt-cutters, and I used them to cut the lock off an access gate to the South side of the Barnwell Regional Airport. As had generally been the case so far in our journey west, the place seemed neglected and deserted. The native grasses had reclaimed anything not fully paved, and weeds grew up through any available crack in the pavement.

I couldn't see either of the two runways listed in a pilot's guide I brought with me, just in case. The guide showed the full layout of the airport, including the location of all the hangars. That was my destination. As we neared these buildings, we came upon a series of now derelict aircraft, tied down on the weed choked ramp in various states of disrepair. They were useless for my purposes. I needed a whole airplane in flyable condition, and old enough to not have been affected by the electronics destroying EMP that we suspected had initiated the current state of affairs. What I really wanted was a small, two place airplane which could be hand propped to start the engine, as the batteries had surely long since been depleted, and couldn't power an electric starter anyway. Something like a Taylorcraft, Stinson or Piper Cub would be perfect, but there just weren't too many of these venerable airplanes still flying.

We first went to one of the main hangars, and were able to break in though a side door. My flashlight beam revealed three business jets, two Cessna Citations and a Lear. They appeared to be in perfect condition, but like the four Cessna 182s which shared the hangar, they were worthless, trapped in the hangar by huge bi-fold doors which could only be opened by their electric motors, now inoperable without the power being back online.

So, we continued outside, walking down a line of T-Hangars which housed smaller, mostly single engine aircraft. Cutting each lock in turn with my bolt-cutter, we discovered only newer and larger airplanes than I was looking for, but on the ninth one in line I hit the jackpot. When I pushed open the hangar doors, I was greeted with the vision of a Piper J-3 Cub, dusty of course, but apparently in perfect condition. We fully opened the doors, and after pumping up the tires using our foot pump, pulled the airplane outside.

Washing it down was out of the question, but with shop rags from the hangar we removed most of the dust which covered the wings, tail, engine cowling and fuselage. If I could succeed in getting her started and airborne, the slipstream would quickly blow the rest away. I examined her closely, and determined she must have been recently restored because the engine was immaculate, minus the dust, and the fabric covering the airplane was Ceconite, not the linen which was used when the airplane was first manufactured. Ceconite doesn't rot over time in a humid climate like South Carolina. It was painted the classic Piper Yellow with a black stripe. I just hoped I wouldn't wreck this classic airplane. I hadn't flown anything in over fourteen years, or a Cub in nearly sixty.

When I expressed these concerns to my wife Dottie, she looked me in the eye and said "It's time you got back in the air, it's your natural environment and I know you've missed it." "And one more thing honey, I'm going with you. What happens to you happens to me. We're joined at the hip and share a brain, remember?" "Besides, you will need an extra set of eyes while you're up there, it's going to be reconnaissance, right?" As much as I tried, I couldn't come up with a rational argument to deny her wish. If we did go down, it would be together. That was getting ahead of myself however, first I had to get it running.

We laagered at the airport that night. It rained hard for several hours, and since I had tied down the Cub on the ramp, our group was able to sleep warm and dry on the T-hangar floor which had been swept clean. The next morning, I woke to clear skies and pleasant temperatures. I walked over to the Cub and was pleased to see that the rain had done what I couldn't do the day before. There wasn't a speck of dust visible. Mother Nature had washed her in preparation to welcoming her back into the sky, or so I hoped.

I had breakfast with the group and then began my pre-flight of the Cub. It's a very basic airplane, with no electrical system at all. It has few instruments on the panel, just an altimeter, airspeed indicator, tachometer, magneto switch and a ball-bank indicator in a glass tube. The fuel quantity indicator is even more simple. It consists of a wire with a loop at the top which is sticking out of the fuel tank cap on the top of the cowling just behind the engine. The wire has a float on the other end, and the fact that it was sticking out of the cap for almost ten inches indicated that the tank had been topped off prior to being hangared after its last fight. The owner knew what he was doing, because a topped off tank precludes moisture forming at the top of the tank and polluting the fuel with water.

I checked, and sure enough the tank was full. I then checked the sump drain at the bottom of tank, draining a few ounces of fuel into a clear plastic cup that I found on top of the instrument panel, obviously put there by the owner to remind himself to sump the tank before flight. This was a careful person. I opened the cowling on both sides, and was pleased to see that everything was in pristine condition. The four-cylinder head covers were shining chrome plated, the spark plug wires looked new, and the oil looked clean on the dipstick. I closed the cowling and made sure the tail and wings were still securely tied down and the wheels chocked. It was time to see if I could get her started.

I put Dottie in the front seat after making sure the parking brake was set. I cautioned her to keep her feet off the brakes and then we discussed the starting procedure. "I will slightly open the throttle. "I said. "Then, I will say 'switch off' and you check to see that the magneto switch is pointing full left to off, and confirm by saying 'switch off'." "I will then pull the prop through several revolutions to get some oil in the cylinders and make sure there isn't a hydraulic oil lock after sitting for so long without being run." "Finally, I should be able to stand behind the prop on the right side, holding onto the strut for balance." "I'll say 'switch on'" and you confirm 'switch on'" after turning the magneto switch full right to the 'L/R' position." "I'll then pull down rapidly on the prop and she should start."

After several repeats of this procedure, the little four-cylinder engine coughed and roared to life. It was the sweetest sound I'd heard for years! That was followed by wild cheering and clapping from the group which was watching the procedure from a distance. Now it was time to get the show in the air!

I got into the seat vacated by Dottie and directed Dave Carson to undo the wing tie downs and tail rope, and pull the chocks. After that, I taxied out to relearn the intricacies of a "tail-dragger" airplane. I would start just taxiing around the ramp, carefully avoiding the derelict airplanes and clumps of weeds which had grown though cracks in the pavement. I didn't want to make the Cub into a large Weed-Whacker and stain the yellow paint with weed clippings. A vanity thing, I guess.

After a few minutes of that, I taxied out onto the longest runway. It must have been resurfaced shortly before the Event, because there were no weeds in view, just tall grass on the sides and ends. I taxied to the end of the runway and proceeded to do some high-speed maneuvers, running the engine up to takeoff power and then traveling down the runway at a speed where I could lift the tailwheel off the ground, but not quite get airborne. After about twenty minutes of these maneuvers, I taxied back to the ramp in front of the T-hangar and shut the engine down to renewed cheers from the group. Tomorrow morning, weather permitting, the Water Lily Air Force would make its inaugural flight. I could hardly wait!

We pushed the Cub back into its hangar, and swept out an empty one two spaces down for us to sleep in that night. Then, we all gathered together for a meeting to discuss what we would do next. The attack in Allendale was obviously fresh in our minds, and we all agreed that we would have to be more vigilant on the road and during our nightly laager if that was possible. In addition, if I was successful in getting the Cub safely into the air and return, we would have "Eyes in the Sky" to map out the best route and avoid any obvious dangers.

I thought about an admonition from my first flight instructor, a seventy-year-old World War One aviator. "Never forget that takeoffs are optional, but landings are mandatory!" He said with a straight face. "It's better to be down here wishing you were up there than up there wishing you were down here!" "Never takeoff into bad weather or wind conditions you can't handle." I never forgot that, and in a nearly fifty-year flying career, I had never "Bent a piece of Tin". I didn't want to start now.

We got out my AAA road map and surveyed the route I had marked with a green highlighter. It of course was at a scale that only showed the main roads, none of the side roads which we had already used in our travel. Using the Cub for aerial reconnaissance would change that. From even a thousand feet, it would be possible to pick the most direct path towards our next destination, and I could fly lower, much lower, to investigate any areas of concern.

It was decided to try for the vicinity of the town of Windsor tomorrow. Perhaps we could even get as far as Aiken State Park. Two of our slowest walkers would now ride in the Jeep, with Bill Fleming driving and his wife Peggy riding shotgun and tending to our wounded in the trailer. That should quicken our pace significantly. We all bedded down as darkness fell, and with sentries posted went to sleep. I had a hard time drifting off. My mind would just not shut down, thinking about what I was going to attempt in the morning. It would certainly be a big day!

Sunrise was shortly after six AM, full light by six-thirty. Going through all the hangars yesterday we had found a total of six gas cans which held five gallons each. We emptied them and filled all with fuel drained from hangared airplanes. I didn't want any from the ramp derelicts because it might have been contaminated by water. So, I had thirty gallons of aviation fuel available for the Cub, enough for about seven hours of flight time or four hundred- and twenty-miles total range. There were other airports along our planned route where I could probably get more avgas, but in a pinch the Cub could burn regular auto gas, much more abundant, of course.

The hour arrived, and I put Dottie in the rear seat, set the parking brake, and went through the starting procedure myself. This time the engine caught on the first attempt, and I climbed in and put on my seatbelt and shoulder harness. Dottie had already done the same. Dave Carson and Dan Lewis pulled the wheel chocks and I gave them the traditional salute and started to taxi out to the runway, past a waving crowd of well-wishers. The wind sock hung limp, so I taxied to the end of the nearest runway, the longest, and went through my pre takeoff checklist. The engine ran smoothly, and the magneto check went off within normal parameters. It was now or never. I taxied into takeoff position after checking for inbound traffic. Of course, there wasn't any, but old habits die hard.

I turned to look back and see if she was ready, and Dottie gave me a thumbs up and shouted over the noise of the engine "Lets' go, Flyboy. Show me what you've got!" I shoved the throttle forward, and we started the takeoff roll. At about twenty miles per hour I pushed forward lightly on the stick and the tailwheel came off the ground. I now had complete forward visibility and concentrated on keeping the airplane in the center of the runway using inputs of the rudder. At sixty mph the airplane lifted off by herself, and WE WERE AIRBORNE!!! Dottie hollered "WHOOPEE", and my heart soared with hers. I had done it! But now the real test would come, getting us safely back on the ground. I pulled back on the stick gingerly, trying to maintain sixty indicated on the airspeed. I remembered what my old flight instructor had said. "You only need to remember one number." "A Cub lifts off at sixty, climbs at sixty, cruises at sixty and approaches at sixty." "Flare and pull the power off and she'll touch down at about thirty." Simple, right? Yeah, and a whore is easy to meet!

I decided to do several touch and go landings before attempting to make one to a full stop. So-called wheel landings are the safest method to use until you are completely familiar with your tail-dragger airplane. Using that concept, you touch down at a level attitude, several mph above stall speed, and only lower the tail when you are nearly at taxi speed. Everything went okay. I bounced slightly on the first landing, but the next three were smoother, the best one the last, which was a full stop. I turned the airplane around and taxied back to the ramp. Dottie leaned forward and patted me on the head. "Way to go Captain Al." She shouted. I felt like I was sitting on top of the world. I had done it. The mandatory landing had been accomplished. I remembered one other thing my flight instructor had said. "A good landing is one you can walk away from. A great landing is one where you can re-use the airplane!" I could certainly do that! So, the Water Lily Air Force had completed its first mission, just a test hop, but a vital one. Hopefully there would be many more missions to follow, and all as successful as the first.

After topping off the fuel tank, we prepared for our first airborne reconnaissance. The plan was for the group of walkers to leave first, followed by Bill and Suzi Mason in the wagon. The Jeep, now driven by Bill Fleming, would follow as soon as I got the Cub safely airborne. We would give them a five-hour head start, to save fuel for the airplane. Bill in the Jeep would catch up quickly. I explained that I didn't need a runway to land the Cub, just a straight stretch of road, preferably paved and free of trees or power poles too close to the edge of the road. Into the wind would be nice for the first few days, as I got more confident in my tail-dragger flying skills. I showed Ari how to hold up a brightly colored piece of fabric as a quasi wind sock, so I could judge the wind direction and velocity on the ground as I flew over the caravan. Based on that, they would pick my road-runway using the parameters we had discussed. As we killed time that morning after the caravan left, I decided to make one more visit to the big hangar to see if I could find some aviation oil and filters for the Cubs engine. I found that and more. In a metal cabinet in the shop area of the hangar I discovered a bunch of walkie-talkie radios and a case of AA batteries. They must have used them to contact the line guys out on the ramp. I turned two of them on, and to my amazement they still worked! The combination of being inside a metal cabinet and surrounded by an all metal hangar building must have acted like a giant Faraday Cage, and protected them from the effects of the EMP. We could now communicate with the caravan while we were airborne rather than have to wait until we landed, an incredible bonus! We took all the radios and the case of batteries and loaded them in the jeep. I kept two for the airplane and Bill clipped one to his belt.

After the five hours was up, I fired up the Cub and took off, circling the airport until I saw the Jeep depart and proceed up the road after the caravan. I then followed the agreed upon route, and in a few minutes saw the group on the road ahead. Just for the fun of it, I pushed the nose over and buzzed the caravan at an altitude of fifty feet or so, wagging my wings at them as I pulled up. We had agreed upon that maneuver as a visual sign that everything was okay. I then climbed to a thousand feet AGL and flew on, surveying the planned route all the way to the Aiken State Park, past the town of Windsor. I made it there in minutes, but it would take the caravan another 5 hours to cover the same ground. I descended to five hundred feet, and Dottie began closely observing the route from that altitude, occasionally using the binoculars to study something closer. This was mostly farm country, with lots of forested areas surrounded by fields which had mostly gone fallow. Occasionally, however, we did see a plowed field, indicating that the farmer had a diesel tractor which still functioned. The plowed plots were small however, obviously being used for subsistence farming. We only saw one person, a woman hanging laundry on a clothesline next to a double-wide trailer. Dottie watched her through the binoculars and said she looked up when she heard the sound of our engine, stared for a moment and then dropped what she was holding and ran back into the house. It must have shocked her to see such an airborne apparition after a year of silence in the sky.

I climbed back to a thousand feet and turned around to do an initial survey of the route we would take for the next few days. That completed, I reversed course and again descended back down to five hundred feet for a closer look. Again, it was mostly forests and farmland below, sparsely populated and now seemingly deserted. By the time we returned, the caravan had made it past Windsor and was laagered in a field just short of the Aiken State Park. There was a straight bit of road just past the laager and I got on the walkie-talkie. "Sky One to caravan" I said. "Anyone up on the radio?" "Roger Sky One, I read you loud and clear." It was Ari. "This road should work." He said. "Dead calm down here". "Roger that". I replied. "Get out of the way, here we come."

I did another circuit of the proposed runway, and Ari was correct. There were no serious obstacles to avoid. I did a standard left-hand traffic pattern and landed safely, shutting down the engine as I rolled out. Mission two complete! I helped Dottie out of the airplane and she immediately ran over to tinkle behind a bush. I went over and did likewise when she returned. We turned off our radios to save the batteries, and then Ari and I pushed the Cub off the road and onto the entrance to the field where the laager had been set up. I felt we had some issues to discuss.

First was the difference in speed between the airplane and the caravan. Realistically, the maximum distance our caravan could cover in a day was twelve to fourteen miles. We had increased the average to twelve miles a day, but that was far short of what the Jeep, let alone the airplane, could travel. It was wasteful of our avgas to just have me and Dottie orbiting overhead, so I had a proposal. After a morning flight covering that days expected march and a few miles farther on, I would come back and land. We would then use a rope tied to the tail tie down ring to tow the trailer and the airplane with the Jeep. It would lower the fuel efficiency of the Jeep, but auto fuel wasn't a problem. We could syphon all we needed from abandoned vehicles along the way. If the need arose, I could always takeoff again for another reconnaissance sortie.

The second issue was the security of the airplane. I told the group we should make the nightly laager large enough to keep the airplane safe in the middle. It was an asset we couldn't afford to lose. I also suggested making laager stops at small airports along the way, checking all hangars for avgas and other useful items.

Finally, I told everybody that we should implement the plan to dismantle the travois, and pack all of the walkers and their gear onto the Jeep, trailer and wagon. I again estimated that we should be able to seriously increase our daily mileage that way, not being held to the pace of the slowest person of our group. If we can find a small abandoned diesel tractor to pull the wagon, Bill and Suzi can ride their horses, freeing up at least two seats for walkers. We might end up looking like a wacky version of The Beverly Hillbillies, minus Granny in her rocking chair, but the faster we found our family members, and got to the safety and comfort of the mountains, the better.

CHAPTER XIII

THE BEVERLY HILLBILLIES

How can I describe this? If I was writing a script for a TV movie, it would be turned down as too improbable. I wish I had a picture, but again, we had no working digital cameras or smartphones, so a description, however inadequate, must do. It is the Beverly Hillbillies redux.

Dottie and I took off for our morning airborne reconnaissance the next morning at first light. The air was smooth as glass, and the view we enjoyed can only be described as pastoral. Rolling farm country and forest, crisscrossed by dirt roads and paved ones with only an occasional farmhouse or small town. Lots of churches, of course. This is South Carolina after all, the state with more Baptist Churches per square mile than anywhere else in the country! No signs of life however. Is everyone still asleep, or have they all gone, and to where?

After about forty-five minutes we saw a large four lane highway ahead. That had to be I-20, the main road between Atlanta and Columbia, SC. There were a few cars and trucks on the highway, but not many, another sign that the Event must have occurred in the middle of the night, probably around two or three AM, when little traffic was on the road. As with the rest of our reconnaissance so far, no signs of life were visible. We continued our flight towards Batesburg, the maximum distance we calculated we would be able to travel today with our new caravan configuration. Again, nothing moved on the ground below us.

I circled around Batesburg and headed back to the caravan, this time much lower, for a closer view of the route we could take. That's when Dottie spotted him. He was standing in front of a large church with a very prominent white steeple and waving his arms wildly. I dropped even lower, down to perhaps four hundred feet AGL and went into a steep banked turn around the church. Dottie said that she could see though the binoculars that he was shouting something, but of course not being a lip reader, she didn't know what.

I was concentrating on my altitude and airspeed. I didn't want to stall in the steep turn, as a stall/spin would be unre-coverable at this altitude. Suddenly Dottie shouted "Oh God!" "Watch out!" I looked down to see the man now had a rifle in his hand and it was pointed straight up at us! There was no sound, but I suddenly felt a couple of thuds and saw two holes appear in the right wing, only inches from where we were seated. The bastard was shooting at us! I leveled the wings and pushed on the stick, diving and attempting to make ourselves a harder target. Either he gave up, or his hits were lucky shots, as nothing else hit the airplane that we could see.

I turned to look at Dottie. Her eyes were wide, and I could see she was shaken by the attack. "I'm okay". She said. "I'm okay." She has flown with me many times, both as a passenger on my airline trips and in our own Cessna 182 which we owned for years before I retired. She isn't exactly a nervous flier, but she isn't much for steep turns, etc. Our low-level turn, accompanied by the sudden rifle attack, had clearly left her shaken, whether she admitted it or not. So, I climbed back to a thousand feet and tried to keep everything as smooth as possible on our return flight to the caravan.

By the time we got there the wind had picked up on the ground. Ari was standing on a dirt road which bordered our laager site, holding the improvised cloth windsock above his head. It was standing straight out, and clearly favored a landing on that road. I contacted him on the walkie-talkie, and he said "There's just a four-foot barbed wire fence about twenty feet off either side, you should be fine". "Okay." I said. "This turned out to be our first combat air patrol". "What happened?" He replied. "I'll tell you on the ground". I said, and promptly entered my traffic pattern and landed uneventfully.

We sat there in the airplane for a few moments after I had shut the engine down, composing ourselves. "You sure you're all right?" I said. "I can get someone else to be my observer". "No way Jose`." She said. "We're in this together, to the end, one way or another". I just sat there in silence, shaking my head as Ari walked up the road to talk to us. Putting my wife of fifty years in danger was not part of my flight plan, but I knew her iron will would not let me change her mind. We indeed were in this, until death did us part.

"Okay." Ari said. "What's this about a combat air patrol?" I just pointed to the holes in the wing and said "Got any duct tape?" "Shit!" He exclaimed. "What the hell happened?" I explained our encounter with the churchyard shooter, and he went off in search of that universal repair item, the roll of duct tape. With it I covered the entry and exit holes in the right wing with carefully trimmed two-inch patches. Their grey color would be a permanent reminder of the possible danger which lurked below. We were lucky in several ways. If the bullets had passed through the floor of the Cub they would have easily gone through the padded seats, seriously injuring or even killing one of us. In addition, if we had been flying a more modern aircraft like our Cessna 182, the bullets would have gone through the fuel bladders, which are located in the wing roots near the fuselage. At best case we would have had an unrepairable fuel leak. At worst case the bullet could have ignited the fuel and we would have been blown out of the sky. The fuel tank in the Cub is mounted in the fuselage just behind the engine, a smaller target, but still vulnerable. I must try to think of a way to better protect it and the seats in the future. One thing for sure, we weren't going anywhere near that church on the way through Batesburg.

While we were gone, the ten travois had been disassembled and stacked, half on the trailer and the other half in the wagon. Dan and Pat were now fully on the mend, and said they could sit up with no problem. That made room for some of the items carried on the travois, and we distributed the rest in the trailer and wagon. There wasn't that much really, so all the walkers could now ride, either on the Jeep, or sitting on the sides and back of the trailer and wagon. Piled high but moving faster, the Beverly Hillbillies caravan was now on the way. The Jeep and trailer went first, followed by the airplane, being pulled backwards by a rope attached to its tail tie down ring. This unlikely trio was followed by the horse drawn wagon. Again, I wished I could take a picture.

Dave Carson, our former Army Ranger and point man, now rides standing in the Jeep. Supported by the roll bar, and with legs spread apart, he looks like a tank commander standing on the turret of his tank. He is wearing his bullet proof vest, and has his AR-15 hanging across his chest, ready for instant action should the need arise. Dave always has his thirty round magazines taped together Special Ops style. So, he is capable of putting sixty rounds on target very rapidly if necessary. He is absolutely someone you want as a friend, not an enemy.

We can make an average four miles per hour at the new pace, probably double what we did when we were mostly walking. If we can find a working vehicle to tow the wagon, we can move even faster, as the horses, now ridden by Bill and Suzi, would be able to vary between a walk and a trot, averaging something like seven to eight mph on fairly level ground. The mare and stallion are young and very fit. Resting to graze every couple of hours, something like fifty miles per day for them wouldn't be out of the question.

The day's trek begins, and we are all impressed at the amount of ground we are covering. We are going though relatively flat farm land right now, on a good paved road. The few farm houses we see are set well back off the road, and none show any signs of life from a distance. We don't make any attempt to approach any of the dwellings. If people are in there, we will leave them alone, and just pray they will do likewise with us as we pass by.

All went well before the noon lunch break, we had to stop and hand push the Cub through some areas where the trees were much closer to both sides of the road. In one area in particular, we had less than a foot clearance total, but made it past without any damage to "Water Lily One", the Cub's new nickname. We proceeded through more open country in the afternoon, and by the end of the day were about eight miles south of Laurens, SC. We had gone over forty-five miles, an incredible pace considering how far we had been able to go as a walker caravan. The question was, as always, could we keep it up?

By my calculation, we were roughly forty miles from my daughter's house in Greer, SC. If we keep up todays pace, we would be there by late tomorrow afternoon. At first light, Dottie and I would make the reconnaissance flight for the day. We were coming up on the heavily populated areas of Greenville and Greer, and I didn't want us to blunder into a bad situation because of lack of planning. Were there still bands of looters or even armed militias in that metropolitan area, a full year after the Event? I had no way of knowing.

We took off into a cloudless sky in the morning. It was cool and calm, and we were eager to make the short flight up to Greer and fly over Megan's house. Was everything all right there? Was she, our son-in-law Matt, and our two granddaughters Vicki and Faye safe and well? We had no way of knowing, but would soon find out. Again, an eerie stillness prevailed below us as we flew northeast, over the towns of Laurens, Fountain Inn and Simpsonville. A few abandoned cars and trucks, but no human activity to be seen.

We saw I-85 straight ahead, and then the Greenville-Spartanburg airport with its long runway and terminal. Several airliners were at the gates, but again no human activity around them. We turned left and followed the road leading to Megan's community. As we approached it, we were horrified at what we saw. Many of the homes were just charred shells, virtually burned to the ground. We were able to pick out her home by the wooden fence I had helped them build a few years back, as well as the location of the sandbox and patio.

The house was still standing, but a portion of the fence had been knocked to the ground. Looters? I descended to just over two hundred feet above the ground and circled the area so Dottie could get a better look through the binoculars. "The sliding door is broken." She said. "Get closer, there's something painted on the garage door, but I can't make it out." I dropped down another fifty feet and continued to circle the house. "The cabin in the woods!" She exclaimed. **"THE CABIN IN THE WOODS!"** "Oh God, I think they've tried to get to Bill's Mountain!"

CHAPTER XIV

THE NOTE - BILL'S MOUNTAIN

When we landed back at the laager, I called a group meeting to explain what we had found. I told everyone that I believed we should stay where we were for another night so I could make another reconnaissance flight which would take the group, by back roads, completely around the Greer area to the East, avoiding all formerly heavily populated sections of the city. If we were caught there by another group like we had encountered in Allendale, we could be in real trouble. Then, I explained where I was going to try and guide us. To a place called Bill's Mountain, in the area of Lake Lure, NC. Prior to the Event, we had spent at least one month every summer at a beautiful house on the mountain, owned by a wealthy individual who had rented it to me for a token fee for the past few years. How that arrangement came about is a long story, but I'll try to explain as briefly as possible.

After I had retired from my airline career, I had spent four years flying for an air ambulance company based in Albuquerque, NM. I flew various models of Beech King Airs, which were a perfect fit for the demanding terrain and short runways in the four states surrounding the "Four Corners" area of the Southwest. The company had a rotor wing and a fixed wing division. The helicopters handled anything which was less than one-hundred miles from Albuquerque, and the King Airs covered everything else, and also when the weather was IFR. The fixed wing pilots used to joke that the helicopters were grounded by a heavy dew!

One stormy night we got a call from the hospital in Silver City, NM. There had been a bad automobile accident, and the two occupants of the car were both in bad shape, one with extremely critical head injuries that the hospital staff there were not qualified to handle. It was snowing outside, and when I checked the weather in Silver City, it was just barely above landing minimums, with heavy snow and gusting winds. Not a great night to be flying. I was sixty-one years old at the time, and our operation was single pilot IFR certified. There would be no co-pilot to help with the navigation or radio work. As always, I was on my own.

I called my medical team and told them the situation. It was going to be dicey, but I figured we could get there and make the approach and landing if the weather didn't deteriorate further. They knew me. I wasn't going to put their life in danger, or mine either, but the accident victims very lives might depend on whether we could bring them back to the

University of New Mexico Hospital in Albuquerque, which had some of the best brain surgeons in the Southwest. My flight nurse and EMT loaded all the items they would need, and we took the King Air 200, which had two stretchers not one, which was the case with the other King Air models. I called the tower and explained the situation. They allowed us to stay in the hangar till the last possible moment and then be pulled out, start up and quickly taxi and takeoff, before the snow could adhere to the wings and tail surfaces.

The flight to Silver city was uneventful. I climbed high enough to be above the snow storm which raged below us, and were cleared direct to the Silver City Airport, being a "Lifeguard" air ambulance call sign. The weather there had indeed deteriorated. There is no control tower at the Grant County Airport, and the lowest approach at the time needed a minimum of a three-hundred-foot ceiling and three quarters of a mile visibility to land. The AWOS was indicating that the weather was below that level, with a three-hundred-foot ceiling, but only a half mile visibility in blowing snow. Not promising. I set up the approach and told the medical team to buckle up. This could be a rough one! They in turn contacted the ambulance on the ground and told them we were on approach.

On my first attempt I flew down to the MDA and leveled out, watching for the approach lights below. When I reached the DME missed approach point I couldn't see a thing and had to pull up and go around for another attempt. The same thing happened on the next approach. As I was coming around for another, and last attempt before I'd have to proceed to my alternate airport, I asked the med team what they wanted me to do. They were nervous after the two misses, but said to give it one more try. The patients, at least one of them anyway, were in dire shape. They needed our help. I set up for the approach and hoped for the best.

At the MDA, it was very rough. I was hand flying the airplane and trying to keep it as smooth as possible. The DME slowly counted down, and just at the last second, I saw a glimmer of the approach lights and continued my descent, breaking out at about two hundred and fifty feet AGL with the runway in sight. Touching down with a strong crosswind, I cleared the runway and rapidly taxied back to the ramp. The door was open, and the flagman allowed me to taxi all the way in to the nearly empty hangar and shut down the engines.

I had plenty of fuel for the return flight, so I just helped the med team set up the ramp to load the stretchers, and went into the ramp office to file my return flight plan and check the Albuquerque weather. It was awful, snowing harder than when we left, and just at the lowest minimums I was allowed for the approach, a two-hundred-foot ceiling and a quarter mile visibility. At least it was going to be a full ILS approach, with localizer and glide slope. I was going to be a tired puppy when we got back to Albuquerque, as I had already been up over fourteen hours, and had many adrenaline bursts from the three difficult approaches into Silver City. "I'm getting too old for this." I said to no one in particular.

I returned to the airplane and helped load the patients. The woman was first, and she looked very bad. Her face was swollen almost to the point of being unrecognizable as being human, and she was almost completely covered in gauze dressings. She was completely comatose, and had that foul odor which the human body emanates when it begins to shut down. It is a precursor of death. Her husband came next. He was heavily bandaged, but awake. He weakly grasped my arm as I pulled his stretcher into place. "Thank you for coming. Please save my wife." He said weakly. I gently patted his arm. "We will." I said. "Just hang in there!" He nodded and smiled, and then closed his eyes. I dearly hoped I could keep that promise. His wife looked and smelled as though she was at death's door. We closed the door, were pushed out of the hangar and started the engines. I quickly taxied out and took off into the snowy night. After contacting Albuquerque Center, we were cleared direct to the Albuquerque International Airport. It was going to be a race with death.

We contacted Albuquerque Approach Control, and I informed them we had an extremely critical patient on board. They immediately diverted several other aircraft which were ahead of us in line, and cleared me direct to the outer marker. It was then that "Murphy's Law" came into effect. I noticed a low oil pressure light illuminate for the left engine. I looked at the oil pressure gauge, and the pressure had dropped to zero. I quickly feathered the propeller and shut down the engine. Unbelievable! Now I was going to have to make a single engine approach to minimums in blowing snow and a maximum crosswind. Why me Lord? I thought.

I told the approach controller what had happened and declared an emergency. He told me to contact the tower, and added a final "Good luck." "You are cleared to land, runway eight". Said the tower controller. "Ceiling two hundred feet ragged, visibility one half mile in snow and blowing snow."

"Your choice of turn if you miss the approach, left or right. The equipment is standing by." All this was said in the typical non-emotional voice ATC controllers always have. They are pros. I doubt anything can fluster them. "There won't be a missed approach I said." "It's all or nothing on this one." "Roger." He said, adding another "Good luck". I was going to need it.

With about ten miles to go I turned on the wing lights. The ice was beginning to build up on the leading edges. Great! Another fly in the ointment. The airplane couldn't handle a load of ice. Especially at this altitude, and on one engine. I turned on the de-icing boots, and hoped they would break off what had already accumulated. I could feel the presence of the "Grim Reaper". He had just taken a seat on the tail and had a big grin on that skeletal face. Five clients coming up!

Everything on the instruments were lined up, localizer and glide slope. I put out the first notch of flaps, but waited on the landing gear. That was just too much drag on one engine with an iced-up airplane. "Please God, don't let me forget to put it down at the last minute." I prayed. I called up the EMT and told him what was going on. He was a big guy, a moonlighting fireman, brave as they come, but his face was white as a sheet, or so it appeared in the reflected light from the instrument panel. "Hang on tight, I'll get us there." I said. He squeezed my shoulder and went back to strap in. He was just along for the ride, and he knew it.

At one hundred feet above minimums I put the landing gear down and selected full flaps. We were committed now for sure. The next hundred feet took forever, or so it seemed. At the two-hundred-foot minimum altitude, nothing, no runway in sight. I continued down, and at just under one hundred and fifty feet AGL we broke out of the clouds. That beautiful fully illuminated, one hundred-fifty-foot-wide, Fourteen-thousand-foot-long runway stretched out in front of me. We had made it.

My passengers both survived their injuries. The gentleman turned out to be an extremely wealthy Swiss businessman who owned extensive properties all over the world, including one on Bill's Mountain at Lake Lure, NC. He had asked many questions after he fully recovered, and learned of the efforts I had made, both to get on the ground at Silver City to pick them up, and also to make the critical single engine approach at Albuquerque International which saved all our lives. He later contacted me, and said that if there was ever anything he could do for me or my family in the future, not to hesitate to contact him. He gave me his private telephone numbers as well. Over the years since the accident we had become friends. Dottie and I had visited him and his wife Genevieve several times at their palatial home in Lausanne, Switzerland, and then made use of his unique "off the grid" mountain estate property on Bill's Mountain in North Carolina. Little did we know that this relationship would turn out to literally become a life saver in the future.

So, that's how I met our benefactor, Bernhard Klaus. He allowed me and/or my family to use his Bill's Mountain home for at least a month each summer. After he grew older, he rarely visited the property, but made it plain that it would be properly maintained, and always available to us with very little notice. I was given a full set of keys for the place, and knew its workings quite well. At Bernhard's urging, I made another set for my daughter Megan and my son-in law Matt McClintock. Bernhard made it clear that they had equal privileges to use it as well. My Granddaughters Vicki and Faye, loved being there, and it was a standing joke to call the seven-bedroom, eight-bathroom estate house the "Cabin in the Woods", which Vicki had dubbed it, after her first visit when she was three years old.

That was where I hoped they had gone, after leaving the cryptic message painted on the garage door of their now abandoned house in Greer. We would fly there in the morning, and see if they indeed were in residence at the mountain retreat. Dottie and I slept little that night. We had once again been given hope for their survival, and didn't want to see that dashed to pieces by reality. Our launch was set for first light, and we would carry two of the walkie-talkies with spare batteries wrapped in Styrofoam, towels and duct tape. We would drop the bundle if we saw them, with a note attached to explain their use.

We took off as scheduled, and in about forty-five minutes were approaching the site. It was at the very top of Bill's Mountain, where a ten-acre spot had been cleared, and the main house, barn and stables, plus several other substantial outbuildings had been constructed. There were two acres of pleasant grass lawn and a full half acre under cultivation, with grape vines and lots of space for fresh vegetables to be planted. It was reached by a mile-long dirt road off a paved side road in the valley. Every effort had been made to disguise the entrance, which had a metal gate that couldn't be seen from the road at all. There was no mailbox, and even when the place was in use, the grass was allowed to grow up to above bumper level of anything lower than a jacked up pickup truck. Food, supplies and visitors had always been flown in by his helicopter based at the Greenville-Spartanburg airport, and parked in the same hangar which housed his Gulfstream G550 Business Jet when he was in town. There was of course a lighted helipad onsite. The road entrance was rarely used, and uninvited visitors were obviously discouraged.

Out of caution, I flew around the valley below the mountain, constantly circling, apparently at random, as I worked my way towards the compound. I didn't want to bring the attention of any unwanted observers to its location. As we passed overhead in another circle, Dottie cried out "I can see them, I can see Megan and the girls!". I continued on, and then made several more circles farther on, before turning back and descending to about one hundred feet above the treetops. Dottie was ready with the radio bundle, and we dropped it squarely in front of the main house and then flew on, starting to make more random circles several miles down the valley.

We both were listening to the radio when Megan's voice came in loud and clear. "I knew you'd find us daddy. I just knew it!" She said. "But it took so long, we had about lost hope." Megan is forty-three years old, but I guess I'll always be "Daddy" to her, and she'll always be our "baby". "Are you alright?" Said Dottie. "Is Matt there?" "Yes". Megan said. "He's down with our friend Kevin fishing for our dinner." How long have you been here?" Asked Dottie "About three months." Said Megan. "It took us over a week to come here from Greer. We had to travel only at night." "Oh daddy, there are awful people down there. They're doing terrible things."

"It will take our group a couple of days to get here from south of I-85." I said, we'll be taking all back roads and avoid all populated areas." "Please be careful daddy. Like I said there are terrible people, dangerous people, around Greer." "Don't worry, we'll be careful." I said. "There are twenty-two of us, and we're well armed." "I may fly over the area again tomorrow, but not right over the house. I don't want to bring attention to you until we're there and can fort up. We're good at that honey." With that comment, I signed off and turned back towards the laager. We would soon be on our way into the hills.

CHAPTER XV

INTO THE HILLS

As I flew back to the laager site, I pondered Megan's words. "Bad people, awful people, doing terrible things". She was clearly frightened, but of whom, and where were they located? I realized I had made a bad mistake by not asking for more details over the radio, but I didn't want to call attention to their location once we had found them. Hopefully, my attempt to conceal what I was really interested in on Bill's Mountain had succeeded.

Megan had mentioned their "friend" Kevin. Had he made the dangerous trek from Greer with them, or had they met him up there, or on the way? Were there any others up there with them, and how well were they all armed? There were just too many unanswered questions, and they probably would remain so until our caravan succeeded in reaching the sanctuary offered by the off the grid estate. Did I say "off the grid"? Hell, there WAS no power grid anymore. Anyplace which could produce its own electricity would have become prime real estate in anyone's book. Something people would be willing to kill to acquire, or do likewise to defend. I felt a new urgency to get to Bill's Mountain as quickly as possible, but what dangers lay ahead?

When I landed at the laager site Ari was the first to come over and discuss the days mission. He was delighted to hear I had found my family, apparently safe and unharmed after the ordeal of the last year in Greer. Everyone soon gathered around Dottie and me, and the questions came hard and fast. How did the compound look from the air? Had I seen any other people besides Megan and my granddaughters? Had I found a good route to get there, and how long did I think it would take the caravan to make this leg of our journey? I answered as best I could, but finally begged off, saying that Dottie and I needed something to eat and drink.

After a respectful delay, Ari came to where I was sitting. He touched my shoulder, and silently beckoned me to follow him. When we were out of hearing distance of the others he stopped and turned around. "Something has come up." He said. "I thought you should know, before I tell the others." Since Ari wasn't prone to secrecy, my interest was immediately aroused. "What happened?" I said. "Well, just after sunset last night, I thought I heard something." "I had climbed to the top of that little hill over there to look around." "There was a slight breeze from the northeast, and suddenly I heard it." "Heard what?" I said. "Well I can't be sure, it was very faint, but could swear that it was the 'Maghreb', the Muslim call to prayer at sunset". "And one more thing." "The words weren't Arabic, I speak that very well, many Israelis do. I swear the

Maghreb was being chanted in Farsi." I just stared at Ari for a few seconds while all this sunk in. "Farsi?" I said. "You think it was being sung by an Iranian?" "I know it sounds crazy." Ari replied. "And I haven't heard anything else today." "Maybe it was just that last night the conditions were perfect, but I'm sure I heard it." "You were already asleep when I came down from the hill, and I didn't have a chance to tell you in private before you left on your morning flight. I didn't want to spook the others."

What next? Could there actually be a Mosque in the area which was dedicated to the Shia sect of Islam, and weren't the majority of Shiites from Iran? We had encountered very few people in the nearly two hundred miles we had covered during our trek so far. Would a group of people who had survived the Event really want to call attention to their existence by loudly chanting prayers several times a day? I put this question to Ari. "Devout Muslims pray five times a day." He said. "Starting before sunrise and ending before retiring to bed at night." "It is a serious lapse of faith to miss one of these prayers, so yes, if they are here, they must follow those rituals." "I understand." I said. "We have to tell the others. These people might not be a threat to our group, but we have already learned that we have to be wary of everyone, including an old man standing outside a Baptist church!"

I called a group meeting, and we all sat around discussing the events of last night and this morning's reconnaissance. Like Ari, everyone was overjoyed to hear that I had found my family members alive and well. However, they were also troubled to hear the warnings we received from Megan after we dropped the radio and she was able to converse with us.

I didn't sugar coat anything, but told them exactly what she had said. Then Ari got up and told about hearing the Muslim call to prayers last night. There was much discussion about this, and the possible effect it could have on the rest of our journey as we transited the Greer-Spartanburg area. Then Jack Swanson raised his hand and stood up.

"We all remember the news stories about wealthy Saudis establishing Madrasas in this country to teach the Wahhabi sect of Sunni Islam to children. These schools were the basis of small compounds of Muslims which were very secretive and kept the general public away using armed guards at the entrance." "I knew there were reportedly several in South Carolina, but I wasn't aware that the Iranians, who are primarily Shia Muslims, were doing the same thing." "We all know the antipathy that the Iranian Mullahs have for America." "Death to America is one of their mantras." "I think we should do all in our power to avoid these people if we encounter them.

Then Dave Carson stood up. "I've read a lot about the Iranian Mullahs and the version of Shia Islam they preach." He said. "The most radical among them believe in the 'Mahdi', the so-called Twelfth Imam." "They teach that when he returns it will signal the end of the world as we know it, and only the faithful, his followers, will be reborn in paradise." "These 'Twelver Muslims' are extremely dangerous zealots. God help us if they've got a foothold around here."

These comments brought silence as everyone digested what had been discussed. I stood up and told everyone that we had to be very careful from here on out until we reached the safety of the Bill's Mountain compound. I proposed that we proceed with extreme caution. Today, we would only travel about ten miles, laagering tonight in the open area just northeast of the Greenville-Spartanburg airport. Then tomorrow morning I would do one more reconnaissance flight, and with luck we would reach the compound by late tomorrow afternoon or early evening. The meeting broke up, and we loaded up the 'Beverly Hillbillies' caravan and got on our way. Traveling slowly, we got to the planned site and set up our defensive laager. That done, I took the bolt cutters and my AR-15 and cut a hole in the chain link fence which surrounded the airport. I wanted to have a look around.

The Greenville-Spartanburg airport has a very long runway for an airport its size. Its eleven-thousand-foot length is long enough to accommodate the largest jets, and had been built with the thought in mind to have an extensive air cargo operation utilize the facility. There were a couple of UPS Airbus freighters sitting on the cargo ramp, and I could see in the distance several airliners on the ramp in front of the terminal, a Southwest 737 and a Delta MD-80, both still connected to the building with jetways. I wasn't interested in them. My destination was the large hangar owned by Bernhard Klaus. It was on the other side of the airport, directly across from the terminal building, so I had nearly a mile walk to get there, straight up the runway. Dave Carson had volunteered to come with me to watch my back. We made it a point not to let anyone stray too far from the group alone. No sense in taking any unnecessary risks.

I hoped that I would find shortwave radio equipment in the hangar, and that like the walkie-talkies we had found in Barnwell, the metal construction of the hangar had protected them from the effects of the supposed EMP. We got to the hangar after about a thirty-minute walk and I used the bolt cutters plus a small sledgehammer I had brought along to break the lock to the side door of the hangar and gain entrance. There was some light available from skylights in the roof, so we didn't need flashlights, which I foolishly forgot to bring. The large hangar was empty except for the Klaus helicopter, a couple of small tugs to move larger airplanes around, and to my amazement, a C-47, the military version of the venerable civilian DC-3, in the D-day paint scheme, olive drab with white and black 'victory stripes' on the wings and a painting of a sexy blond labeled "My Gal" on the forward left side just under the cockpit. It sat next to a bright red Piper "Super-Cub" back in a corner. The Super Cub had an electrical system and a starter, but could be hand propped as well if they didn't work. If I could figure out a way to open the hangar doors, we had an addition to the Water Lily Air Force. A plane which was faster, and could carry more weight for a longer distance. It might even be possible to get the ancient warbird in the air, who knew? But first things first. Where were the radios, if they existed?

I found a functional flashlight on a workbench in the back of the hangar and began searching the interior rooms. The third one I opened was crammed with radio equipment of all types, including, I noted, short wave radios. However, if none of them were battery powered, they were useless. But then I had a thought. This was a Bernhard Klaus facility, and he was one of the most precise and careful men I had ever met. Attention to detail was everything to Bernhard. A Swiss trait, I assumed. That small nation had not survived for hundreds of years surrounded by potential enemies without careful thought and planning for the unexpected. Had Bernhard insisted on a backup electrical system for his hangar? Knowing him I couldn't imagine he hadn't.

I went out behind the hangar, and sure enough, found a large Caterpillar brand diesel power generator of the type many grocery chains use to power their stores electrical needs during power outages. Would it start? Was there any fuel remaining? We'd soon find out. I checked inside the strong metal battery box and found four large deep cycle batteries, but did they still hold a change? A press on the starter button answered that question. After a couple of turns the engine turned over and ran smoothly. The volt-ammeter showed full power. We were in business! Back inside, the lights were on, and I went immediately to the radio room. I turned on the shortwave radio and noted there was a sheet posted on the wall which had various frequencies listed. One said "Bill's Mountain". I spun the dial to that frequency, and broadcast in the blind, hoping that Megan and Matt were monitoring the radio up there. They had plenty of power from the solar powered electrical system, and I knew there was also a big diesel-powered backup system for use during cloudy days if the batteries were discharged.

"Dad to Megan and Matt. Dad to Megan and Matt. Do you read me, over?" At first, I heard nothing but static, so I repeated the message several more times. Suddenly, a voice came over the speaker. "Hi dad." It said. "This is Mike, and I read you loud and clear, how me, over?" I was so flabbergasted I almost couldn't speak. How could our son Michael, the other member of the Farragut family who lived in South Carolina, possibly be with Megan and Matt on Bill's Mountain?

"I read you loud and clear, but how in the hell did you get up there, over?" "It's a long story dad. I've been with Megan and Matt since about 2 weeks after everything went down. First in Greer, and now up here, when we had to leave their house after everything went to hell in a hand basket down there, over." "God, it's good to hear your voice. We have a lot to talk about when we get there. I hope it will be by late tomorrow. Can you give us any pointers?"

"Just be very careful." He said. "There are a bunch of crazy Muslims killing all non-believers on sight. They think it's the end of the world or something." "They're between Greer and here, and they go out hunting people like animals. Like I said, they're nuts!" It was what Dave Carson had said. This was a bunch of 'Twelvers', and they were cleansing the world of infidels in preparation for the return of the Mahdi. We would

somehow have to get past them and on to the safety of the Bill's Mountain compound, but how?

"Okay Mike." I said. "I can't wait to tell your mother you're alive and well. She will be ecstatic!" We're camped just outside the Greenville-Spartanburg airport, and I'm in Bernhard Klaus's hangar. I'll fill you in on that we get up there." "I'll make another recon flight in the morning. Just me. I'll leave your mother behind. With less weight I'll be able to climb higher and get there faster. I'll look for the Muslim compound to see the best way to avoid it." "I'll call on the walkie-talkie when I'm close, but I won't fly directly overhead. Listen up, I'll be airborne just after dawn, over." "Okay, dad, we'll be listening in the morning, but for God's sake be extra careful. Those guys have automatic weapons. AK-47s I think, and they must have plenty of ammo, because we hear them shooting all the time. I love you dad, over." "I love you too Mike. Hug Megan and the girls for us. With a little luck we'll all be together tomorrow night. Over and out."

Tomorrow would possibly be our last day on the road for a while, perhaps forever. However, before we could reach the sanctuary of the compound, we would have to pass through what might prove to be the most dangerous territory we had traversed thus far. We bedded down at sunset. Shortly thereafter we all heard the unmistakable sound of the Muslim call to prayer, which was repeated several hours later. None of us would sleep well tonight.

Just before sunrise we heard it again. It had to be amplified, but how far away was the sound coming from? There was no way of knowing. Over Dottie's protests, I prepared for my first solo reconnaissance flight. I took off at first light, and circled over the airport to gain altitude before heading towards the Lake Lure area and the compound. I was surprised at how much better my rate of climb was without Dottie on board. She doesn't weigh that much, something like a hundred and forty pounds, I'd guess, but it did make a difference. I leveled out at seven thousand feet, which was something like fifty-five hundred feet AGL. I headed north-northeast following a country road on the south side of I-26. The route bypassed the small towns of Inman and Campobello and finally crossed I-26 just south of Landrum. I hadn't seen any sign of a Mosque with the traditional minarets so far, but I kept looking.

I could now see Lake Lure in the distance straight ahead. As I got closer the ten-acre cleared spot on top of

Bill's Mountain was clearly visible. Suddenly, I heard "Is that you dad?" Over the radio. I chuckled at that. How many airplanes a day passed overhead since the Event? "Water Lily One checking in. How are things going down there? Over". "We're okay". Mike said. "Just worried about you guys getting here safely. Has the caravan started yet?" "No". I said. "They wait until I get back with my reconnaissance report." "Well maybe they should wait until dark to start." He said. "We've been hearing a lot of machine gun fire in the last few days, but only during daylight hours. Those bastards don't hunt people in the dark, I guess." "I understand." I said. "But I have to guide them to you with the airplane. We don't have any accurate maps of the area, and I don't want them to get lost." "We tow the airplane behind the Jeep to save gas after I get back. Depending on what I see, we may have to make one more stop tonight, to get inside of twenty miles from the compound. Then I can lead them in from the air in the morning." "Okay, but keep us advised if you can." He said. "From that close, we might be able to hear you with the walkie-talkie." "Remember you're in really bad territory now, those guys are bloodthirsty murderers." "We'll be careful". I replied. "we're well armed. Not fully automatic weapons, but we still have a lot of firepower at our disposal. Talk to you later. Over and out".

There were scattered clouds below me, but suddenly I caught a glimpse of a large white building with four towers at the corners. The Mosque was located in a secluded valley. I could only see one dirt road leading to the compound of buildings which surrounded the structure. There had to be a lot of people living there if they had been able to grow their own food after the Event. A small river ran down the valley, so fresh water wasn't an issue. The clouds quickly obscured my view. Had they seen me? I was pretty high, but they probably did hear the sound of the engine. The airport was dead ahead, and I decided to land on the long runway. Hell, it was my private strip for now, wasn't it?

I had an idea. Thunderstorms were building in the west, so why not cut a large enough opening in the fence around the airport to allow the caravan to go to the Klaus hangar? We should be able to open the hangar door using the generator, and everyone can keep safe and dry before we start the final part of our trek to the Bill's Mountain compound. It was obviously going to be dangerous, and we needed to have a long meeting to discuss what we were going to do.

That was agreed upon, and the caravan moved the mile and a half to the front of the hangar. We fired up the generator, and with some trepidation I found the open and close buttons for same. When I pressed the green button labeled "UP" the door slowly opened. I stopped it with just enough room for the highest object in the caravan (the wagon) to pass under it, and then closed it again. I didn't want a curious observer (if there were any in the vicinity, drawn by the sight of the Cub landing) to know we were in here. Then I shut down the generator to save fuel and eliminate the noise of its diesel engine,

The whole group was excited to see the C-47 and the Super Cub, especially since I said the old warbird could easily accommodate thirty passengers plus two pilots if I could get it up and running. That was more than we had in our group plus the people currently at the compound. The only consideration was whether we had anyplace to fly which was safer than here?

The generator had charged up the backup batteries for the radio room, so I decided to call the compound and get some more information. I turned on the shortwave, and once again broadcast in the blind. "Dad to Mike, Dad to Mike. Do you read me, over?" A short pause, and I did it again. This time my son-in-law Matt replied. "Mike's taking a shower. How can we help you, over?" "I just need to ask some questions. When everyone there is ready, call back on this frequency. I'll be standing by, over". "Okay, will do." Came the reply. I sat down and wrote some questions on a note pad on the radio room desk. Since Ari and Dave Carson were there listening, I asked them if they had anything else they wanted to ask Mike or Matt. "I'd ask how many of the Twelvers are there in that compound, does he have any idea?" Said Ari. "And have they ever attacked anyone after dark?" Added Dave. "Okay." I said, I'll add that to my list.

In about five minutes Mike, Matt and their friend Kevin Landry were at the transmitter.

Basically, I learned that Mike and Kevin had been on a hunting and fishing vacation at Kevin's parents private hunting reserve in the North Carolina mountains when the Event occurred. Their truck wouldn't work, but Kevin's four passenger ATV did, and that's how they got to Megan and Matt's place in Greer. There was no reason to stay at the reserve, since Kevin's parents were on vacation in Australia, where they came from. They were both well-armed, having a Mauser hunting rifle and an AR-15, both equipped with red dot sights. Kevin had a scope for his Mauser as well. They also had 9mm Glock handguns to administer the coup de grace to any deer who weren't killed outright on the hunt. These all came in handy when the looting and rioting got totally out of control in the months following the blackout, and in the escape to the Bill's Mountain compound. Finally, the question about the Twelvers came up,

"Well it's hard to say". Said Kevin, with his Australian twang. "Hundreds for sure, and they hunt in groups from just a couple to over a dozen" "More vicious than a Bushmaster, and damn near as hard to kill!" He continued. "Don't think they're afraid of the dark, but they seem to be back at their Mosque by sunset" "That's why we hid by day and only traveled at night on the way up here." Said Matt. "The girls slept in the back of Kevin's ATV and Megan rode behind me on my motorcycle. I had installed an oversized muffler, so it is really quiet. Same for the ATV, don't want to scare off the game, you know." "I understand." I said. Maybe we should leave after dark tomorrow and try to cover as much distance as possible before we have our hidden laager before sunrise". "I can make one more recon flight at dawn, and if the way is clear, lead the caravan to the hidden entrance to the compound."

"Sounds like a good plan dad." Said Mike. "We'll be down by the gate waiting for you when you get close." "Just keep as quiet as possible during the day. They have hunting parties out all the time after sunrise, and they're not looking for deer." "Keep trying to contact us with the walkie-talkies. We'll be listening up." "Okay." I said. "We'll hunker down here in the hangar until tomorrow evening, and give you one

more call just before we leave. Stay safe. We're on the way."
"For sure dad." Said Mike. "You too. Over and out."

We had our meeting and decided two things. First, that speed was essential, so we had to leave the horse drawn wagon behind. It had become our slowest transportation component and now carried mostly non-essential items, like the disassembled travois, canned goods and water containers. There was plenty of food at the compound. Bernhard had a bomb shelter built there at the height of the Cold War, and its storage room was packed with freeze dried food which would last for years. We'd keep all our freeze-dried food, but take it out of its bulky containers and just pack the light-weight Mylar packets into every nook and cranny in the Jeep and trailer. It would be a little tighter packing those who were riding on the wagon on the remaining two vehicles, but we only had something like forty miles to go before we got to Bill's Mountain, and again, speed was essential. Bill and Suzi would ride the stallion and the mare.

The final decision was that Dottie and I would remain at the hangar with the Cub after the caravan left tomorrow night. At dawn the following morning we would takeoff and fly low, almost at treetop level, and search out the fastest route to the concealed entrance to the compound. We'd then fly back and land on a road next to the group and give them as detailed a hand drawn map of the route as possible. We would then all hide in the woods during the day, making the final sprint to Bill's Mountain in the late afternoon, with us once again airborne, leading the way. It all sounded so simple, but then shit always happens, doesn't it?

CHAPTER XVI

"KHODA BI HAMTA AST"

All went off as planned. When Dottie and I got back from our final reconnaissance flight, and landed, eager hands pushed the Cub off the side of the road next to the forest and covered it with precut saplings, effectively camouflaging it from prying eyes, at least from a distance. We all sat around while Dottie and I showed everyone the map we had drawn. There were many references to buildings and landmarks. We didn't know the name of the various side roads, but there were only three turns to make along the way, and we would once again be airborne, talking to Dave Carson in the Jeep to lead the way. It should have been a piece of cake. But then one of those things happened that make "Murphy's Law" stories come true.

When nature calls, we must answer, and all of us had become used to squatting to do our business behind a bush after digging a "cat hole" with a small entrenching shovel that we carried in the trailer, with a roll of toilet paper on the handle. Not very dignified, but necessary. Charlene Davis, our resident Southern Belle, was most fastidious about this process, and had insisted on bringing one of the folding gardening stools along on her travois for the purpose. It was a small thing, and if she was willing to carry the extra weight, so be it. When we dismantled, and finally abandoned the travois, nobody complained when she put it in the trailer. We were close to sanctuary, and it wasn't worth making it an issue. Charlene is a VERY feisty lady when she puts her mind to it. So, in the late afternoon when she went to get the stool and shovel, it was business as usual.

Charlene always went farther away from the group than anyone else when she had to answer the call. To say that she was shy about the process would be a gross understatement. So, when she walked over to the next grove of trees, maybe four hundred feet away, no one thought anything about it. What happened next would shock us to our core, and change the relationship between various members of the group forever.

A burst of machine gun fire, followed by the sound of men yelling in a foreign language brought us all to our feet. "khoda bi hamta ast!" They shouted. "khoda bi hamta ast!" It had come from the tree grove where Charlene had gone to do her business. "Shit! That's 'God is Great' in Farsi." Said Ari. He grabbed his AR-15 and Dave and I followed suit and ran in that direction. We burst into the trees and around a large bush to be confronted by a horrible and shocking sight. There in front of us lay the body of Charlene Davis, face down on the ground with her pants and panties around her ankles. Blood flowed onto her ever present pearl necklace from a series of bullet holes in her back. Her murderers, both holding AK-47s, stood a few yards beyond her. It all happened so quick. Ari raised his AR-15 and began firing at the attackers. Dave and I did the same. They didn't have a chance to raise their weapons before they were both riddled with multiple shots to their torsos. We stopped firing, and as the saying goes, the silence was deafening. We heard running footsteps behind us, and a group of armed men from our group came around the bushes. In the lead was Don Davis.

"Charlene!" He screamed. "Charlene, oh my God. No, No, NO!" He dropped his rifle and ran to her body, turning her over. We were now staring into her lifeless eyes and the ugly exit wounds in her upper torso. She was naked from the waist down, so Ari took off his jacket and covered her up out of respect. Don kept hugging her body, sobbing "No, No, NO!" Over and over. Dave Carson put his hand on Don's shoulder and said "Come on Don, we've got to get out of here before their friends show up. We'll take care of Charlene." He pulled away at first, but then slowly turned and looked directly at me. "You caused this." He said quietly. "YOU caused this. We should never have left our homes". Suddenly he lunged up at me, a look of pure hatred in his eyes. "YOU KILLED HER!" He screamed. "YOU DID IT!" "SHE'D STILL BE ALIVE IF WE HADN'T ALL GONE ON THIS CRAZY TREK! IT WAS ALL YOUR IDEA!"

I stepped back as Ari and Jack restrained him. He had a point, but in fact, Charlene had been one of my greatest supporters. She knew we had to leave the Low Country. It was just a matter of time. Don was the husband, but Charlene was the dominant one in the marriage. "What she says goes." Said Don on a regular basis, and he meant it. But grief is a strange thing, and it was obvious that Don had forgotten all that. His hatred was now focused on me, not Charlene's killers, and that could turn out to be a real problem in the future.

Ari went back to the laager and returned with two blankets and a machete. We used that to cut down a couple of straight saplings and made an improvised stretcher. We gently picked her up and placed her on the stretcher after we had pulled up her panties and shorts to restore her dignity. Even in death she would have been mortified to be seen in the state we found her. Ari gently closed her eyelids, and we covered her with the extra blanket and returned to the caravan. Don was being consoled by a group when we arrived. We placed Charlene in the trailer and then went to the center of the group. "We've got to get out of here, and NOW!" Said Ari. "There have to be more of those bastards around, and we can't get caught in the open."

Everyone loaded up, with two of the smallest women now riding double behind Bill and Suzi, to make extra room in the trailer for Charlene's body. They immediately departed, with the Jeep and trailer in the lead. I fired up the Cub, and Dottie and I took off, flying low over the column and giving Dave Carson directions over the walkie-talkie. Even flying as slowly as possible, I still had to constantly circle back so they could keep us in sight. I figured we now had about twenty miles maximum left to go, and they were keeping up a good pace. If all went well, we should be at the turnoff for the compound in about two and a half hours. As I led them onto the last stretch of road which would lead to the compound, I decided to circle back towards our departure point to see if we were being followed. I informed Dave and Ari of my plan, and then descended to about one hundred feet AGL. Even at only sixty mph we would make a hard target.

Not hard enough, as it turned out. About twenty minutes after leaving the caravan we were passing over a small stretch of woods when I felt a series of thuds and heard Dottie scream. "They're shooting at us!" "Get us out of here!" She said. I banked hard to the left and dove for the treetops, leveling out just above them. No more bullets hit the fuselage, but there was a new set of holes on the underside of the right wing, farther outboard than the ones made by the church shooter. Worse, I saw that several bullets had gone through the right tire, making jagged holes in the rubber. This was going to be a tricky landing for sure.

I flew back to the caravan, finding it now less than a mile from the last turnoff. Mike had been monitoring my conversations with Dave, and broke in to say that He, Matt and Kevin were on the highway, waiting to lead us into the dirt road up to the compound. "How bad are you hit dad?" He asked. "Any control problems?" "No." I replied. "I don't think they hit anything serious, just more holes to patch. I think I'm going to put myself in for an Air Medal!" Mike laughed at that comment, and then said "Where are you going to try to land it?" "Well, if I land it down on the highway, it will probably be discovered and destroyed. I'm going to look at landing it on the compound grounds. I only need about four hundred feet to get it stopped. Is there that much area cleared in a straight line?" I asked. "Sure, you've probably got twice that, and the wind is dead calm now." He said. "Wait until we get the caravan to the top of the mountain, and then I can check for the best spot." "Okay." I said. I can see you now. The caravan is only about a mile back. I'll orbit above the compound until you're there and check things out myself. Thanks."

It took about another forty-five minutes to get the caravan safely up the mountain with the hidden gate closed behind it. I had all that time to pick my spot. Now all I had to do was get this wounded bird safely back on the ground. Mike agreed with my chosen landing zone, and I gently set her down on the left wheel, keeping the damaged tire off the ground as long as possible. However, when I could no longer hold it up, it touched down hard. The tire immediately came off the wheel, and the Cub ground-looped to the right, lightly touching the right wingtip, and ended up facing the opposite direction we had been going when we landed. I shut down the engine, and we were immediately surrounded by a dozen cheering people. We had made it! We had made it safely to the sanctuary of the Bill's Mountain compound! All of us but one, that is.

I looked out at Don Davis. He was standing next to the trailer with his head bowed. His right hand was touching the blanket wrapped body of his wife. He was only about fifty feet away, and when he looked up and stared at me, the expression on his face was contorted with rage. I now had an enemy in the group to deal with. How would I manage that? I had no idea.

CHAPTER XVII

SANCTUARY

After over a year of bathing with a washcloth and a tub of water warmed over a fire, the sensation of taking a hot shower, all lathered up with soap, was amazing. The simple pleasures of life, a hot cup of coffee, or feeling really clean, had become luxuries. All of the seven bedrooms in the house were en-suite, with their own full tub and shower. Solar panels on the roof heated the water, which was then stored in a very large, extremely well insulated tank that could maintain the temperature using electric rods that got their power from electric solar panels or even by the large diesel-powered generator when necessary. So, seven people at a time were able to get clean. We would be a much better smelling group at dinner tonight. But we weren't getting clean and changing our clothes for that, we were going to a funeral.

Ari suggested that we follow Jewish custom, and bury Charlene the day after she died. Like many things from the

Talmud, such as not eating pork or shellfish (because trichinosis was common in biblical times and the hot climate of the Middle East meant that shellfish not quickly consumed after it was harvested from the sea could spoil, releasing deadly toxins) the practice of rapid internment of the deceased meant that a body would not begin to decompose in the desert heat prior to burial. It was also Jewish tradition that the soul of the dead person could not rest until the body was buried.

Janet Lewis and Peggy Fleming had carefully removed Charlene's bloody clothing, bathed the corpse of their friend, and then dressed her, even tidying up her hair and applying some makeup to conceal the death pallor which always occurs in the deceased. They washed the blood from her ever present pearl necklace, and then put it in place around her neck for the funeral service, which would take place that evening. With the help of several of the men, Charlene's body was placed on a makeshift bier at the front of the large media room which was on the first floor of the house.

We all filed into the room, and Ari, now dressed in his Rabbinical garb and wearing a Yarmulke, sang a soulful song in Hebrew, followed by readings from the New Testament, since Charlene had been a staunch Southern Baptist. Several of the group stood and eulogized Charlene, and finally Rachael, Ari's wife, sang a beautiful rendition of "Amazing Grace" to the sobs of many of us present, especially Don Davis. At the conclusion of the service Charlene's body was placed in a simple casket, which had been built with boards we found in the stable, and then taken to the large walk-in refrigerator located in the basement of the house, where it would remain until burial the next morning. Don was inconsolable, and constantly stared at me with a look of pure venom in his eyes. Would that irrational hatred ever end? That was anyone's guess.

The funeral went off without a hitch, the burial as well. I purposely stayed in the background. Obviously not because I didn't like and respect Charlene, but because I didn't want to intrude on the grieving process which was now under way, especially with Don Davis, who for whatever reason blamed me for her death. Perhaps that was a bad choice on my part, but I would have to live with that. We had dug the grave on the side of the hill which had a beautiful view of Lake Lure and the imposing rock face of Rumbling Bald Mountain behind it. Everyone but me tossed a symbolic handful of dirt on the coffin after it had been lowered into the grave, and Ari read the English Burial Service, ending with the traditional *"We therefore commit her body to the ground; earth to earth, ashes to ashes, dust to dust; in sure and certain hope of the Resurrection to eternal life, through our Lord Jesus Christ."* This read by a Jewish rabbi, from Charlene's small, King James Version of the New Testament Bible. Four of the men then filled in the grave, and Don Davis wept as he placed a small bouquet of wildflowers on Charlene's final resting place that my daughter Megan had picked, with the help of my granddaughter Vicki, that morning. We would carve a headstone as soon as we could.

Although it was a somber group eating dinner that night, the food was the best we had enjoyed since the boar meat barbecue we'd had at the Mason farm. Megan, Matt and the girls shared one bedroom, so there were six other bedrooms

available. It was unanimously decided to give one to Bill &
Suzi Mason because of her condition. The remaining five
were assigned to couples by a raffle. Mike and Kevin volunteered to sleep in the bomb shelter, as did the raffle losing
couples, Dottie and I among them. We had several sleeping
rooms down there. The bunk style beds were not fancy, but
comfortable. Don Davis chose to sleep in a tent next to Charlene's grave. Our enemies were out there, and in unknown
numbers. So, for our continued safety we maintained the
same watch schedule we used in the nightly laager during our
trek up here. For the time being, Don was removed from the
watch rotation. Both Ari and I agreed that he wasn't mentally
stable since Charlene's death.

After the burial, I called a meeting. Everyone but Don
Davis attended. I said that we must do a complete inventory
of the available resources at the Klaus estate. What we discovered over the next few days was extraordinary. Bernhard had
obviously wanted his Bill's Mountain estate to be a refuge
from a "Nuclear Winter" should World War III break out
when he and his wife were here in North Carolina. I wondered if he had similar setups in his other properties around
the globe. The bomb shelter was a wonder unto itself. It was
buried under ten feet of earth, and I calculated that it had at
least six feet of reinforced concrete forming the roof and side
walls. The entry door was an inch and a half thick and made
of high-quality steel. It opened and closed using hydraulic
operated pistons powered by electric pumps. It could also
be operated by hand cranked pumps in an emergency. All
air to the shelter was equipped with an air filtration system
which could supply clean air under the harshest conditions

imaginable, filtering out radiation and poisonous gasses. The outside vents were located hundreds of feet away, in apparently undisturbed woods, and disguised to look like boulders. There was also an escape tunnel nearly three hundred feet long, which ended at another entrance, also equipped with a steel door, but disguised to look like one of the rock formations which dotted the surrounding landscape. The shelter and the house had separate deep wells as their water supply, free from contamination or destruction by outside forces. As I have mentioned before, Bernhard Klaus is a very cautious man.

The rest of the shelter was a marvel. It was basically a ten thousand square foot building with ten-foot-high ceilings, divided up into many rooms, all of which had poured concrete walls and heavy steel doors which rendered them virtually soundproof. Five sleeping rooms had bunk beds similar to what I had seen in documentaries about our atomic submarine fleet. Each "bunk" was actually a self-contained cubicle which had a thick accordion curtain for privacy, and storage cabinets built into the wall. It also had a small flat screen TV which could show a vast number of movies which were stored on a large database computer. The cubicles also had built in reading lights and individually controlled heating and air conditioning.

There was a substantial armory, which contained a variety of automatic and semi-automatic rifles, all in the NATO 7.62 mm caliber, as well as a large selection of handguns. A quick estimate indicated that there were over one hundred thousand rounds of rifle and handgun ammunition. In addition, there was a large stock of C-4 plastic explosives and detonators. You could fight a small war with what this room contained, and we might have to do just that.

The kitchen was equipped with every modern cooking convenience, and had a large walk-in refrigerator and equally large fully stocked freezer. While the refrigerator was empty, the freezer could probably feed all of us for over a year without ever using any of the large quantity of canned goods and freeze-dried foods stored in the huge pantry. All this was over and above the matching facilities in the main house. Food at least, was not going to be a problem for quite a while.

The main house, as described, consisted of seven en-suite bedrooms. They were on the top two floors of the three-story house. The main floor had a huge kitchen/great room with a large fireplace at the far end with floor to ceiling windows on each side, which gave a beautiful view of Rumbling Bald Mountain and Lake Lure below. There was also a very large formal dining room and of course the entertainment center, with the largest flat screen TV I had ever seen. It had to be over one hundred inches diagonally.

At first glance you would think the house was frame built, but we discovered from the plans, located in the basement, that it indeed was also reinforced concrete covered with a concrete based ship lap siding with a special metal layer which had shielded the homes electronics from the effect of the suspected EMP. Everything functioned perfectly, without exception. The roof looked like wood shingles, but indeed was also reinforced concrete with concrete shingles that appeared to be random wood in nature. The special metal barrier protected that as well. Hell, I imagined that you could napalm the place and not feel a thing!

The aforementioned basement contained a large workshop, a walk-in freezer and refrigerator that were twins of the ones in the bomb shelter, another armory, similarly equipped, and a large diesel generator which backed up the solar panels on the roof. There was a five-hundred-gallon hot water tank and a complete radio room, also duplicated in the shelter. All the exterior and interior doors appeared to be wood, but were in fact heavy steel, so perfectly balanced that my two-year-old granddaughter Faye could easily open and close them. There was one other unique feature. The windows were all inch-thick bullet/bombproof glass similar to what was installed in the White House. More Bernhard Klaus precautionary measures. This "home" was indeed a nearly impregnable fortress.

In our yearly summer visits, we had of course noticed some of this, the thick steel doors, the extra thick windows, etc. However, the doors to the basement and shelter were marked "Private", so we didn't intrude on Bernhard's private places. We were just glad to have such a wonderful place to stay for a few weeks, away from the summer heat and humidity of South Carolina's Low Country. The other outbuildings in the compound included a ten-stall stable and barn, well stocked with high quality dried hay, plus oats as fodder for the horses. In the stable storeroom there were large stocks of veterinary medicines. The stallion and mare would be well cared for. Finally, there was a substantial shed which housed several diesel tractors and farming implements, as well as six ATVs which we had previously used for trail rides through the mountains. There were gas station style pumps for both diesel and unleaded fuel. Knowing Bernhard, I assumed they were attached to sizable underground tanks. The question was, how long would that fuel, properly stored and filtered, remain useable? I'd have to look into that.

The final discovery was that the entire unassuming fence which surrounds the inner ten acres of the compound is, or at least could be, electrified. That might come in handy in the future, but for now, I felt it was unnecessary. Also, Bernhard had CCTV cameras hidden all over the property outside the inner compound. You could sit in the entertainment-media room and view the entire estate, all the way down to the gated entrance off the highway. To my amazement you could also view the interior and exterior of the Klaus hangar at the Greenville/Spartanburg airport. The cameras down their must operate on long life batteries, perhaps recharged by solar panels. Bernhard had thought of everything, it appeared, but even he could not have imagined the evil which was headed our way.

CHAPTER XVIII

REVELATIONS

The next morning, I got up early and decided to get a cup of coffee and then examine the radio room of the shelter more closely. Cup in hand, I turned on the lights to reveal a ten by fourteen-foot room which was crammed with radio equipment. There were VHF and UHF radios, several impressive CB base stations, several short-wave radios and finally a couple of what appeared to be satellite communications devices. Everything seemed to be there in duplicate. More Bernhard penchant for order and backup capability.

There was a red three ring binder on the desk label "frequencies". I opened it, discovering a much more elaborate list than had existed in Bernhard's hangar at GSP. There was a separate page for ten different locations around the world, but the most extensive list was for the Klaus estate in Lausanne. The first thing I tried was the satcom radio, to no avail. Next, I tried the big shortwave set, getting nothing but static on the first two listed frequencies I selected, using the station identifier stenciled on the front of the transmitter. On the third frequency, loud and clear, a voice answered. "Identify yourself." He said. I did so, and he replied "Stand by one". A long five minutes passed, and then Bernhard came on the line. "Al, is that really you?" He asked. "Affirmative." I said. "We're at your Bill's Mountain place." "Thank God." He said. "Is Dottie and your family with you? Are you all safe?" "Yes, even my son Mike, and I've brought another twenty-two others here as well. Do you know what happened over here?" That's when I got the news that would shock all of us to our very roots. "Yes, I know exactly what happened, and it's not just there in North America. Over ninety percent of the world has been blacked out for over a year."

Ninety percent? What was Bernhard talking about? I couldn't imagine how so many EMPs could be deployed at once, and who could have the capability to do something like that. I asked those questions, and Bernhard began to provide the answers. "The Iranians attacked the United States using nuclear devices which were part of the North Korean low orbit satellite system." He said. "They thought they could hide the attack because of the recent increase in solar flare activity. What they didn't count on was that there would be a series of CMEs so severe that except for a few slivers of the surface of the planet which were at the terminator when the CMEs occurred, the rest of Earth took the full brunt of the flare activity. In effect, most of the planet is for all intents and purposes back to the horse and buggy days of the nineteenth century." "What the hell is a CME?" I asked. "I guess you could call it God's answer to the theory we have all gotten too dependent on technology, and forgotten our roots, especially our spiritual ones." Bernhard said. "It will take time, but I will fill you in on everything I know, and you have to let me know what is happening over there." "Okay." I said. "But let me contact you in an hour. I have others who must hear what you have to say. Is Genevieve and your family okay?" "Yes. She and they are fine. We Swiss were better prepared than most. I will expect your callback in an hour. Out"

I went and found Ari, Dave Carson and Jack Swanson. I told them I had something important to discuss, and would meet them in the shelter radio room in an hour. They were intrigued, but didn't ask why. Especially since the death of Charlene Davis, I didn't want to overstep my bounds as our elected leader. I knew the irrational behavior of Don Davis was having an effect on the group, and I didn't want to cause further problems if I could avoid it. We were safe for the time being, but that could rapidly change, and we had to be able to stick together as we had done for over a year since the Event.

When the hour was up, the four of us gathered around the shortwave transmitter. I had closed the heavy steel door so we wouldn't be disturbed. When Bernhard came on the frequency, I introduced him to Ari, Dave and Jack. I then explained what had happened to us in Happy Valley over the last year, and of our decision to make the trek west, finally ending up at the Bill's Mountain compound. I thought he would be shocked by my account of the devastation we had experienced. He wasn't. "It's the same in virtually all of Europe." He said. "We Swiss are a bit more fortunate, having developed a sort of paranoia over the years which made the whole country into what is now being referred to as "preppers". In the late nineteenth century, the Swiss government began building immense underground fortifications to defend us from attacks by our neighbors, particularly the Germans and Italians". "Those fortifications, carved out of solid granite, protected a lot of our infrastructure from being damaged by the CMEs. Much was affected, of course, but the computers controlling our water supplies, electrical grid, and even our cellphone networks survived unscathed." "Not so with our neighbors, unfortunately, chaos reigns there." "To keep us from being overwhelmed by looters and worse, Marshall Law was declared, our borders were closed, and the entire Swiss military, including reserves. Were activated."

"Please tell my friends about the Iranian EMP attack on our nation." I said. "Of course." Said Bernhard. "From what I have been able to determine, they thought they could explode two small nuclear devices which they had purchased on the black market in 1990 after the fall of the U.S.S.R. They had made a deal with the North Koreans to trade oil for the use of two of their missiles which were capable of placing satellites in low Earth orbits which would pass overhead the United States multiple times each day." "These two satellites were timed to simultaneously pass just inland from both coasts at least twice daily. They just had to time the explosions to correspond with the arrival of a Coronal Mass Ejection's radiation. That's what CME stands for. It just might have worked too, but the timing was just a little off, and NORAD deduced whose satellites had exploded overhead. They fired missiles in retaliation, and as the saying goes, most of North Korea now is "flat, black and glows in the dark". The CIA and other intelligence agencies including Russia and China had heard rumors of the alliance between Iran and North Korea, so when the EMP attack occurred, Iran suffered the same fate as their ally, and Russia and China were not about to start a nuclear conflict over these two rogue nations." "Then unfortunately, as you Americans are fond of saying, 'The Shit Hit the Fan!'.

"During the next twenty-four hours, four more massive CMEs occurred on the surface of the Sun, and with the exception of a few small slivers of territory along the Terminator, the world was plunged into an electronic abyss. Anything electrical in nature not thoroughly shielded was destroyed by the radiation, which was harmless to life forms but deadly to anything controlled by a computer chip." "I have been studying the phenomena for the last year, and I can tell you where civilization, as you have previously known it, still exists."

To say the least, we were stunned. Ninety percent of the world's population basically moved back in time to the eighteen-eighties? It was almost inconceivable. "Are you still there?" Asked Bernhard. "Yes." I replied. "But what you have just told us will take a bit of time to digest, let alone accept." "I understand" He said. "Perhaps I can move that process along for you. Look at the wall behind you. "We all turned and there on the wall was a ten-foot-long, four-foot-wide Mercator Projection map of the world. It had a series of red push pins stuck into it. I noted that one was located in North Carolina, approximately at our present location, and another in Central Switzerland. I realized these must be the locations of Bernhard's properties worldwide. "Do you understand how a Mercator Map works?" Asked Bernhard. "Well, basically."

Said Ari. "It's kind of like you peeled the skin off an orange and laid it flat on a table. It makes all the parallels of latitude have the same length as the equator, and allows lines of longitude to cross all parallels at a ninety-degree angle, which makes seaborne or airborne navigation much simpler."
"Correct." Said Bernhard. "But the farther you get from the equator, the more distorted the image becomes, so places like Alaska, Greenland, Siberia and Antarctica, although in fact huge, appear much larger than they really are."

We could all see what he was referring to as we studied the large map on the wall. "So, what you can do," He continued, "is put that weighted string you can see on a pushpin on any location worldwide and the string will show you what other locations fall along that line of longitude." "Because the Earth is tilted on its axis, you adjust that area by roughly twenty-four degrees left or right depending on the day of the year and time of day and you'll get an idea of what areas were not affected by the CMEs."

"The four most severe CMEs occurred during the twenty-four-hour period before and after the vernal equinox on March twentieth last year, so virtually no adjustment for axial tilt is necessary. The terminator was running almost parallel to the lines of longitude. The radiation from the most severe CME hit the Earth at seven-thirty PM on the twentieth, and the next three hit seven, twelve and twenty-two hours after that. Since we know that the speed of the Earth's rotation at the equator is one thousand thirty-eight mph, we can calculate exactly where the terminator was at that point in time. I will give you those points with reference to a large city on or near that longitude. the EMPs were detonated at two AM on the twenty-first." "Unfortunately, because of the Iranian EMP explosions, I believe that all of the U.S, as well as parts of Southern Canada and Northern Mexico are totally blacked out if their computer chips weren't properly shielded." Bernhard proceeded to give us those locations, and we marked them on the big map. "Now, Al, I have a private matter to discuss with you if the other gentlemen don't mind." He said. And with that, the conference ended, and I told Ari, Dave and Jack that I'd see them later in the day. They all thanked Bernhard and left the room. "Please put on a headset." Said Bernhard. "Do you see the covered toggle switch on the upper left side of the transmitter." "Yes." I said. "Well, turn that on, and then change to the frequency underlined in red in the book and contact me on that. I'll explain after we're there."

We reestablished communications on the new frequency, and Bernhard said: "We are now speaking on an encoded frequency. Our voices are being scrambled so no one else can hear them." "Why is that necessary?" I asked. "For the simple reason that we are now living in a completely different world than that which existed when we last met. The CMEs and EMP attack on your country has changed everything." Bernhard continued. "The countries which had nuclear weapons capability, and the missiles to deliver them are still players, with the exception of Iran and North Korea, which as I said were effectively neutralized by your country after the EMP attack. I believe that China, France, Great Britain, India, Israel, Pakistan, Russia and your country still have missiles in protected silos that are capable of obliterating the planet if enough countries used them. Right now, no one will. Chaos reigns. Not a single country had properly protected themselves against the EMP or CME threat to their infrastructure, so even though they still retain the ability to start a nuclear war, the rest of their military capacity is in shambles."

"I can imagine what you have experienced over the last year. The same things are occurring all over the planet." "Even in the most stable and conservative societies such as here in Switzerland, the rules of law and common decency began to break down." "Because of who we are, we regained control of our society, but we are under constant attack, not from governments, but groups of individuals who want to take what we have, and are willing to go to any length to get it." "Because of who I am, and my survival instincts, I have allowed good people like yourself and your family all over the world to survive for the past year using facilities like Bill's Mountain, which I had constructed in countries where I maintain residences because of my worldwide business interests." "That can continue for you and for them, but not indefinitely." "We must work together to save humankind from extinction." "So, let's begin. Tell me everything which has occurred in the last year in greater detail. How you survived, and how you got to Bill's Mountain. We must set up a specific time to talk on this frequency each day. Others in my compound here in Lausanne are communicating with my other compounds, but you and I have a special relationship, as Genevieve and I literally owe you our lives, because of what you did for us in New Mexico."

Thus began a conversation which would indeed have monumental implications. Not only for the survival of our little group at Bill's Mountain, but for the remaining population of the planet as well. We had a lot to accomplish, and many challenges and dangers lay ahead. After agreeing on a broadcast schedule, Bernhard and I signed off. I had much to think about, and share with the other half of my brain, my wife Dottie.

Tomorrow would be the start of a long road back, but I remembered the old Chinese proverb: *"A journey of a thousand miles begins with a single step."*

CHAPTER XIX

WHO'S OUT THERE?

During the next few days, Bernhard brought me up to date about who on the planet had escaped the effects of the CMEs. Because of the irregular pattern of the CMEs arrival, the "Free Zones", as we came to call them, were unevenly spaced. The one closest to us ran directly through Halifax, Nova Scotia, almost exactly on the sixty-fourth meridian. That meridian continues south thru Puerto Rico, Venezuela and Central South America. A second Free Zone strangely passed directly through Jerusalem, a third through Central Russia, and a final one through the eastern tip of Siberia and down thru the North Island of New Zealand. Bernhard's people in Lausanne had been attempting to contact people in those zones by short wave radio, but with limited success. There was still a lot of Sunspot activity occurring, but there had been no more CMEs, and the activity seemed to be on the wane, thank God.

Since distance affected signal strength, Bernhard suggested that we attempt to contact people in our hemisphere, particularly those on the sixty-fourth meridian. We were able to have a brief conversation with a "Ham" radio operator in Puerto Rico, but the connection soon went dead. Puerto Rico hadn't had a good power grid even before the Event, and it appeared it would be intermittent now at best. Halifax and other places in Nova Scotia came in loud and clear. We learned that they were faring pretty well, being separated from the majority of the Canada by a considerable distance. They had some refugees arrive by sailboats from as far south as Maine, but apparently not many. The Nova Scotians are hardy people, and between what they could grow during the relatively short season up there, plus the bounty from the sea, no one was going hungry, they said.

During one of our encrypted conversations I passed this information on to Bernhard. "I wish it was so here in Europe." He said. "Unfortunately, it's not. "As I told you, we declared martial law, called up all our army reserves and closed our borders. As the months have gone on since the CME events, we have seen an incredible increase in violent attacks from elsewhere. Mobs of people have attempted to enter our country without permission, and unfortunately some of them have been wounded or killed by our military or police when they wouldn't take no for an answer. People in most of the surrounding countries are dying in ever increasing numbers. Some Swiss citizens who were out of the country on vacations or business when the CMEs occurred took months to walk back home. They brought horrifying tales of looting. People being murdered for a small amount of food, or worse, cannibalism." "Yes." I said. "We have seen the same things here. It is amazing how fast society breaks down when a disaster occurs." "And there is something else." Said Bernhard. "Some of the Muslims, the most radicalized, have gone mad. They, especially the Shias, are convinced that the CMEs, and the chaos which followed, are a sign that the "Mahdi" is coming to cleanse the Earth of Infidels. They have emerged from their European enclaves in murderous hoards, killing all non-Muslims they encounter. Our army fought a pitched battle against a large group of them only last week. They are truly fanatics!"

"Unfortunately, there is a large group of Iranian Shias living in a compound not twenty miles from here." I replied. "They murdered one of our group on the way here, a helpless woman. We killed her two attackers, but I'm afraid the Iranians will be out for revenge if they can find us, and they probably outnumber us by at least ten to one. Plus, they are armed with fully automatic AK-47s and possibly explosives as well." I said. "You must prepare to defend yourselves." Bernhard said. "Have you electrified the perimeter fence? If not, do so, it will slow them down." "You have at your disposal all the materials to make booby-trap devices similar to Claymore mines. You will find a manual which will show you how to make them in the armories in the shelter and the house. I also stocked electronic detonators which can be individually activated by radio control. They can be deadly in an ambush, as your forces in Viet Nam found out when they were attacked by Viet Cong or North Vietnamese Army forces using Russian versions of the Claymore. Have you learned how to use all the hidden CCTV cameras as yet? They automatically revert to night vision after dark." "Yes, we have." I said, "But we didn't know about the night vision capability." "That might come in very handy." Bernhard said. "I'm sure you have discovered by now that I was able to smuggle in a large number of fully automatic weapons as well. They were outlawed by your ATF laws, but I only intended them for use in a situation like you now find yourself in. A total breakdown of society." "There is also a large amount of Teflon coated ammunition, valuable if your attackers are wearing bullet-proof vests." "Do you have any military trained people in your group?" Bernhard asked. "Yes." I said. "Several, including one who was a combat veteran of the Israeli Defense Forces. Another was a Viet Nam era, combat experienced U.S. Army Ranger." "Wonderful!" Said Bernhard. "Get them working on those Claymore style weapons ASAP."

I signed off and found Ari and Dave. I told them what Bernhard had said about the explosives and also about the armored-vest piercing bullets. We in turn found the instruction manual and boxes of ball bearings to use in the improvised Claymores. The munitions factory was now in business. By late that afternoon we had manufactured fifty of the Claymores using the pre-made backing plates with folding stands that ever thoughtful Bernhard had also provided. With radio-controlled detonators attached, we placed them in strategic locations, carefully mapping each with a number. The radio transmitters had one hundred different code numbers, and we could fire them as singles or in groups. The defenses of the Bill's Mountain Compound had been considerably upgraded.

I called another group meeting that evening and told everyone what Ari, Dave and I had been discussing with Bernhard. Everyone attended but Don Davis. He was still living in a tent next to Charlene's grave and avoided contact with all but a very few people. Without Charlene's "Steel Magnolia" personality to guide him, his actions were becoming more and more bizarre. I was starting to wonder if he was becoming mentally unhinged, and as such, a liability to the group as a whole, possibly even dangerous. He was of course, as we all were, fully armed with a rifle and a sidearm. He would have to be closely monitored. When the revelations about the cause of the Event were revealed, it caused a flood of questions. Some wanted to know why they hadn't been informed immediately of the ability to contact other survivors of the catastrophe which had devastated, as they now knew, over ninety percent of the planet.

Dale and Harriet Lawrence, who had been next door neighbors and close friends of Don and Charlene in Happy Valley basically accused me of withholding vital information from the group, and I was disturbed to see others nodding in agreement. Ari immediately spoke up in my defense. "You can't lead by committee." He said. "It just doesn't work that way." "We all elected Al as our leader in Happy Valley, and he has managed to get us safely to this refuge. Unfortunately, all but one. Charlene's death wasn't his fault. We all knew it was past time to leave our compound down there. Charlene, God Rest Her Soul, knew that as much as the rest of us. She knew the risks involved in our trek to someplace safe, but was fully supportive of the concept. She told me that several times, before we left, and on the way here." "If you are dissatisfied with Al's performance as our leader, who is willing to step up and replace him?" The group looked at each other, and then started shaking their heads. I realized I was stuck with the job, like it or not.

I then appointed Ari as my official First Lieutenant and Dave as my Second lieutenant. If anything happened to me, or if I was absent on a reconnaissance flight, Ari was in command. If anything happened to him, Dave was the leader. No one objected to this decision, as it had been de facto in place since we left Happy Valley anyway. I just formalized the situation. We then got down to the business at hand, the manufacturing and placing of the Claymores in the outer perimeter of the compound, and twenty-four-seven monitoring of the CCTV pictures for any signs of a threat, particularly from the 'Twelvers'. I didn't notice Don Davis staring at me through one of the great room windows. Later, I would wish that I had.

The next days were busy. Many volunteers for the two radio rooms, listening to various short-wave frequencies to find out who's out there.

CHAPTER XX

PATROLS

Every army in history has had to send out scouting patrols to determine the location and strength of their adversaries. While airborne reconnaissance, satellite surveillance, and even the use of drones has reduced the use of them, most military commanders still stress the need for "boots on the ground" intelligence. We had Water Lily One as our spy in the sky, but using it would also show them our location if they weren't already aware of it. Something we obviously didn't want to disclose. So, under the command of either Ari Zuckerman or Dave Carson, we began sending out heavily armed patrols to cover at least a 3-mile circle around the compound. It wasn't long before one of those came into contact with an Iranian patrol or hunting party, we weren't sure which, and a fierce firefight ensued. The patrol was led by Dave, and he had his men keep strictly silent, mainly using hand signals or the occasional very low whisper.

This paid off big time, because the Iranians were conversing loudly in Farsi, and our guys set up an ambush, using several of the improvised Claymores and fully automatic weapons loaded with the Teflon coated ammo. It was basically a massacre. Six of the eight-man Iranian group were killed instantly, and at least one of the other two was wounded. That was determined by the blood trail that he left behind. Our guys took all the fully automatic AK-47s and handguns from the dead, plus all the ammunition they were carrying. It was discovered that they also had fragmentation grenades, something which was totally absent from our own armament. That could be a problem in a real full-blown firefight in the future.

Since Dave's Ranger training and Vietnam experience told him that the Iranians were not very well trained soldiers, but rather a militia type organization dedicated to protecting their Mosque, Madrasa and compound, he consulted with Ari, and they came up with a plan to place our Claymores along well used trails where they would cause the greatest amount of casualties without exposing our men to their greater manpower and resultant firepower. This is where Dave and Ari's military training and experience became a Godsend to our little group. Unfortunately, we couldn't follow Stonewall Jackson's Civil War dictum of "Get there fustest with the mostest". We had to outthink and outsmart our enemies or die in the attempt. The 'Twelvers' were religious zealots, and totally ruthless in their methods. There was absolutely no surrender option open to us.

After the initial firefight it was decided to expand the area of our patrols to a ten-mile radius from the compound at least once a week, on Friday, the Muslim holy day. The reasoning for this was they probably wouldn't have anyone in the field on that day, and we could do a more thorough reconnaissance of the area. That turned out to be a mistake. We would use two of the four passenger ATVs from the compound, which would allow the greater distance to be covered in the same or less timeframe. However, although fairly quiet, the ATVs do make some noise, and that noise was heard by a "Watcher in the Woods". The Iranians had placed several of these noise or motion activated cameras to spy on our activities and protect their compound. When they were retrieved, they showed the day and time when our ATVs passed by. When this occurred two Fridays in a row, they planned an ambush. The following week they would be waiting for our patrol.

What saved us from what might have been a disastrous loss was the innate caution built into the training of every U.S. Army Ranger, lessons learned during World War Two and underlined in the jungles of Vietnam. Routine patrols should never take the same route twice, that just invited an ambush. Safety on patrol came from it being completely random in application. When Dave Carson discovered that the Friday patrol took the same route two weeks running, he called all the men who participated in these actions together and explained in detail how they must be planned and executed. So, when the Iranians attempted their ambush the following Friday, our patrol was actually behind them, and caught them in a murderous crossfire. Our guys didn't stick around to make a body count, but they knew it had to have been considerable.

When Dave returned that day, the debrief was very intense. I felt I must take part in these dangerous activities and be a member of the armed patrols. My decision was instantly and completely overridden by the group. As I was the only pilot among us, if I was injured or killed, we would have lost a crucial asset in Water Lily One. As much as I didn't like it, I could see the sense in that argument. However, I had a suggestion. I thought we should trade the J-3 for the Super Cub in Bernhard's GSP hangar. Its larger engine and weight carrying capacity would allow me to take two men, or three women, albeit tightly packed in, on a flight from the compound back to GSP if evacuation became necessary. We must prepare for all contingencies. We planned the swap for the following morning.

At first light Dave and I departed for GSP. The damaged tire and tube had been replaced with the spares I had found in the hangar at the Barnwell airport and placed behind the rear seat. I initially flew away from that airport, circling back over Lake Lure and heading down I-26 to avoid flying over or near the Iranian Compound. We landed about twenty minutes later and I taxied the Cub up to Bernhard's hangar. In a couple of minutes, we had the generator fired up, opened the hangar door just enough to allow us to pull the Cub inside. I then closed the door, and Dave and I walked back to the Super Cub. We pulled it to the center of the hangar and I did a thorough pre-flight inspection. Everything checked out ok and the fuel tank was full. I decided to start it up inside the hangar before taking it outside and returning to Bill's Mountain. The gel cell battery had held its charge and the starter turned over immediately. After about six rotations of the propeller the engine caught and ran smoothly at idle. Everything was go for our departure.

We opened the hangar door and pulled the Super Cub onto the ramp. While I waited in the airplane, Dave closed the door, went out and locked the side door, and then shut down the generator and locked its control box. He ran back to the airplane and climbed in, giving me a thumbs up. I started the engine, taxied out and took off without incident. I again hoped that our activities had gone unnoticed. The flight back to the compound was uneventful. I flew far south of a straight line there to avoid any areas which might contain marauding Iranians. It was the first time I had landed the Super Cub, and only my second short field landing on the compound grounds, but it was accomplished without incident. Many of the group gathered around to see the bright red airplane which replaced Water Lily One. Just for the heck of it, I had three ladies squeeze tandem style into the rear seat and then had two men do the same. It was a tight fit, but if an emergency air evacuation of the compound was required, multiple twenty-minute flights back to GSP would be doable.

We had moved the tractors and farm implements out of their shed, and were now able to pull the Super Cub tail first into the structure, to protect the fabric covered airplane from being damaged by hailstorms, which occasionally occurred up there in the summertime.

Following Bernhard's instructions, we had electrified the outer fence. There wasn't enough voltage to be fatal to someone who touched it, but it certainly would be an unpleasant experience. We had set up a schedule to monitor the CCTV cameras which had been placed all around the outer compound grounds around the clock. I was in constant contact with the person assigned that task by a walkie-talkie, which I carried at all times. Then, late one night several weeks later, I got a call from Dan Lewis, who was on monitor duty. He said that someone was moving in the forest, close to the main gate. I jumped out of my bunk and ran up to the main house. There on the big screen TV was an image of a man with a rifle slung over his shoulder who was carrying a six-foot ladder in one hand and what appeared to be some sort of rug or blanket in the other. We watched as he climbed up the ladder and carefully threw the material over the top of the fence, thereby insulating himself from the electrical charge as he climbed over.

The night vision camera gave a ghostly image of the individual as he tossed his AR-15 over the fence, and the small backpack he had been wearing as well. He then straddled the now cloth covered fence and turned back to look up at the compound in the distance. To our shock, we realized it was Don Davis, and he had a big smile on his face as he turned and slid down the other side, picked up his rifle and gear, and vanished into the darkness.

During the next week neither our daily patrols or the extended patrol on the following Friday turned up any evidence of Don Davis, or even the direction which he had gone. That mystery would be answered in the months to come, and in a way more violent and tragic than we could have imagined. First, however, we would experience a period of peace and tranquility unlike any we had for over a year.

CHAPTER XXI

SUMMER IDYLL - THE FARM

After Dons strange departure, things returned to a state of normalcy at the compound. I can't say they returned to normal, because there was nothing even vaguely "normal" about our lives since the Event. They did however, settle into a routine which lulled us into an unwarranted sense of security. Maybe a false sense of security would be a better way to describe it.

We figured out how the farming implements worked, and that took a bit of doing, since the only ones of the group with any large-scale vegetable farming experience had been Don and Charlene Davis, and they were now both gone. Don had run a large commercial farm in Biloxi, Mississippi for years. It had supplied fresh vegetables to restaurants throughout the south. His help in getting a substantial garden planted would have been invaluable, but since his disappearance, that was not an option.

Fortunately, Bill and Suzi Mason had lived on a farm, and were able to guide most of us city dwellers in what would be required to plant and nurture a garden capable of feeding a group which now included twenty-five adults and children, twenty-six after the coming birth of Suzi's baby.

The farm implements we had found in Bernhard's tool shed included a disk harrow and a seed drill which allowed us to till and plant a half acre in corn, another in potatoes and a final one in tomatoes, several types of squash, including pumpkins, and a variety of leafy greens including cabbage, lettuce and of course the southern staple, collards. Several of the ladies, my wife Dottie among them, became obsessed with weeding and tending our crop as the summer progressed.

With the help of a couple of the men I was able to construct a teeter-totter from scrap lumber and galvanized pipe, and a tire swing from an old tire removed from the small tractor. We hung that from a convenient branch on the massive oak tree at the side of the main house. Soon the air was filled with the giggles and laughter of Vicky and Faye, my granddaughters, age six and two respectively, as they played in the shade of the oak for hours on end. We even converted a shallow horse watering trough into a splash pool for their enjoyment in the warm summer afternoons.

My daughter Megan bonded immediately with Suzi Mason, who was closest to her age of any other female in the group. Suzi was now obviously pregnant; a condition Megan had shared only three years previously. Our R/N "medics", Janet Lewis and Peggy Fleming, kept a close watch on her condition, and assured us that she was in excellent shape as she prepared to deliver her first child. Peggy had let my granddaughters listen to the fetal heartbeat with her stethoscope. After that, Faye would point and inform everyone that "Baby! Baby!" was in Suzi's growing belly.

Bernhard had a fine wine cellar in the main house, and we all took to sitting out on the massive screened in porch with a glass of a vintage to watch the sun set over Rumbling Bald Mountain. Then off to a fine communal dinner prepared by those of our wives who enjoyed cooking. I was grateful that Dottie was among them, as she is my favorite gourmet chef. Bernhard's freezer provided wonderful cuts of beef which had been vacuum sealed and flash frozen to prevent deterioration due to freezer burn. Dave Carson was an avid bow hunter, and that silent method kept us supplied with fresh venison as well. The streams and lakes nearby provided an abundant source of fresh trout and bass to vary our diet. Had it not been for the menace we faced from the Iranians, our current status could have been viewed as an idyllic paradise compared to the last year in Happy Valley.

Since Suzi was forbidden to ride the mare in her current delicate condition, Bill taught Matt and Megan to ride, using the Mason's western style saddles, and to the delight of Vicky and Faye, they would take horse rides around the property on a regular basis, with the girls sitting in front of their parents. One day I caught Faye standing outside the corral looking up at the horses with her arms raised and demanding to be "UP! UP!". She is a feisty little squirt. So, the summer on Bill's Mountain continued without any further strife. We no longer heard the sound of gunfire in the distance, and our daily patrols gave no indication of hostile actions being prepared against us. It all seemed too good to be true, and indeed it was as it turned out.

After he climbed over the fence, Don Davis walked all night and part of the next day. He arrived at the fence surrounding the Iranian compound about three in the afternoon, and began following it from the safety of the surrounding forest until he got to an entrance gate. It was guarded by two bearded men carrying AK-47s. He carefully put his AR-15 and Glock 9mm on the ground, followed by his backpack. He then took off his jacket, shirt, trousers and shoes and socks and stepped out of the forest with his hands in the air and walked towards the guards shouting "khoda bi hamta ast" and "Muhammad al-Mahdi" over and over. To say that the Iranians were shocked to see this nearly naked apparition walking towards them shouting "GOD IS GREAT" in Farsi and also repeating the name of their legendary spiritual leader over and over would be a gross understatement.

Rather than shoot him out of hand, they called the Mosque on their radio, and soon a four seat ATV came roaring down the gravel road leading to the compound. It skidded to a halt and two other dark-haired bearded men jumped out and ran towards Don, who continued his chant unabated. One of the two new arrivals was a good six inches taller than his companions. He had black hair, and a dark complexion like the others, but his eyes were a striking blue color, not dark. He was the first to speak, and it was in English.

"Are you alone?" He said "Were you armed?" "Yes," Admitted Don, "My clothes and weapons are behind the trees back there." He turned and pointed behind him and the blue eyed Iranian, who was obviously the leader, barked a few words in Farsi. The gate guards ran to where Don had pointed and retrieved the items he had discarded. "Are you mad?" Asked the Iranian leader. "Why have you come here?" "I want to join you." Don replied. "I want to convert to Islam!" The leader stared at him for a long moment, and then told him to get dressed. That accomplished, Don had his hands tied behind his back, and was placed in the back seat of the ATV with a guard seated next to him, who pointed his AK-47 directly at Don's heart.

They drove up the gravel road for nearly a mile, much of the time through a heavily wooded area. Then, after passing over a slight rise they came into a large meadow with a small river running through it, and there it was, a gleaming white three-story mosque, surrounded by four slender minarets. To Don Davis, it was breathtaking. The ATV stopped in front of what was obviously the main entrance to the mosque and the blue-eyed leader got out and motioned to Don. "Come." He said simply. The guard seated next to Don unbound his wrists, and Davis climbed out, following the leader as he entered the building. He immediately turned left, proceeding down a long corridor with a large ornately carved wooden door at the end. There was a wood bench on one side. The leader pointed to it and said "Sit," "Wait." And after softly knocking, opened the door, entered the room, and closed it behind him. Don was now quite alone and unguarded.

After a few moments the door opened and the blue-eyed man motioned to Don. "Come". He said. Davis got up and followed the man into the room, which had high ceilings, a plush Persian rug on the floor, and a large desk with two chairs placed in front of it, which, with the exception of the large chair behind the desk, were the only pieces of furniture in the room. The whitewashed walls were decorated with ornate symbols, which Don figured were Arabic or Farsi. Seated at the desk was an old man wearing a tan robe and a black turban. He had a long grey beard and mustache. To Don, he looked exactly like the photographs he had seen of the Ayatollah Khomeini.

"Khoda bi hamta ast", "Muhammad al-Mahdi". Don said. The blue-eyed leader turned and savagely back handed him. Knocking him to the floor. "Do not speak!" He said softly. "Until you are spoken to." "Get up and bow low to the Ayatollah." Don could feel blood flowing from the corner of his mouth, but he wiped it away with the back of his hand and slowly rose to his feet, immediately bending at the waist into as low a bow as he could manage, remaining in that position. He heard the old man say something he couldn't understand, and then blue eyes translated. "The Ayatollah says take a seat." He said. Don complied, and gazed at a face which was both haughty and serene. The coal black eyes seemed to bore a hole into his very soul. Suddenly Don was frightened, what had he done?

The Ayatollah spoke again, and was immediately translated by blue eyes. "He says that you have killed our people, and for that you must be punished." "He asks why you have come here after committing such a crime against true believers?" Don looked at blue eyes. "May I answer him?" He said. "Yes, but be respectful in your tone." Came the reply. "Tell him that I didn't kill anybody. I was only with a group of people who did." Don said. "They held me against my will.

They are very bad people." "I have heard about the coming of the Mahdi. I want to convert to Islam so I can be saved as a true believer." After this was translated into Farsi for the Ayatollah, he looked over at Don. He spoke again and the translation was "I will think on this matter and pray to Allah to give me the truth of what you say. Until I decide, you are our prisoner."

The Ayatollah then rose and left the room by a side door. Don was taken to another building and placed in a room with bar covered windows. It contained a cot, chair, a small table with a copy of the Quran, which turned out to be in English, and a bucket to use as a toilet. Nothing more. Several hours later a simple meal was provided. So far, he was being treated humanely, but how long would that last? Only God, or perhaps more correctly Allah in this case, knew. He must get his story straight, and he had memorized what he was going to say already. He would have his revenge on Al Farragut and all those who supported him, and he would show no mercy.

The interrogations began the next morning, conducted by blue eyes, whose name he later learned was Afshin Javan. He always spoke in a low voice, not threatening, but not friendly, either. Don had been working on his story for several months. Basically, he and his wife were part of a group which had lived in the Low Country of South Carolina in a retirement community called Happy Valley. After the Event they had been forced by their neighbors to give them all the food they processed and to do manual labor to serve them. They had become one step above slaves. These awful people gave them only the scraps left from their meals and beat them regularly. When the neighbors decided they would move west, they had forced Don and his wife to come with them. In the weeks that followed, Don was given more freedom as long as he carried weapons and helped to protect the others. His wife Charlene was kept as a hostage every time he left the group to hunt for food. Because of this, they were unable to escape. When the group attacked two innocent Iranians, his wife was killed when they returned fire trying to defend themselves.

He then told Javan that they had made it to a secure compound on Bill's Mountain, where they planned to hide out until order was restored in the country. He said that he hated and distrusted them, and when he was able to escape from the compound with stolen weapons, he came straight to the Iranian compound to surrender and ask for permission to convert to Islam. He also said he would help the Iranians enter the compound by a secret route only he knew, and kill all the compound dwellers in the name of the Mahdi.

As the weeks went by, the interrogations continued, never varying in content or style. It was obvious they were trying to catch Don in a lie. However, gradually they began to provide him with more literature about Islam, all printed in English, and he was able to ask questions of an English-speaking Imam. One day he was brought several sheets of paper which listed the words and phrases he would have to recite to formally become a Muslim. He was told that he didn't have to do this in front of Muslim witnesses, but could do so if he wished.

So, in early August Don took a ritual shower to cleanse himself of his past life, dressed in a white robe, and stood barefoot before a group of men in the mosque. He recited these words:

"Ash-hadu an la ilaha ill Allah." (I bear witness that there is no deity but Allah.)

"Wa ash-hadu ana Muhammad ar-rasullallah." (And I bear witness that Muhammad is the Messenger of Allah.)

The men assembled all chanted: "Khoda bi hamta ast" (God is Great")

The deed was done. Don Davis was a Muslim convert, and part of the Shia sect of Islam. The next day he and his new comrades began planning the attack on the Bill's Mountain compound.

CHAPTER XXII

BATTLE ROYAL - THE QUISLING

On reflection, we were so naive. We had allowed ourselves to be lulled into a dream world of peace and tranquility which simply no longer existed, if indeed it ever had. I am reminded of a bumper sticker I frequently saw in Happy Valley. "COEXIST" it said, using symbols of everything from the "peace" symbol invented by the Hippies in the nineteen sixties, to the Star and the Crescent of the Muslims, the Star of David of the Jews, and the Christian Cross. I always shook my head when I saw it. What a nice thought, but how does one "coexist" with a group of people who believe that there are only two options in life. Submit to the will of Allah, or die.

Had we known what was being planned, with the assistance of a former member of our group, perhaps we would have been more prepared for what was coming our way, Unfortunately, we weren't. It was going the be a fight to the death. A real "Battle Royal", and we didn't know it.

When Don Davis finally converted to Islam, he brought his own psychoses to a group who already had a sufficient number of their own. Those of us in the Bill's Mountain compound, men women and children, were irrelevant. We were just impediments to the Mahdi's goals. We, like all the denizens of the Nazi concentration camps, were just something to be exterminated, and Don Davis was more than willing to see that happen.

He and Afshin Javan had daily conferences. Don told them of the escape tunnel which led from the bomb shelter to a spot only a few yards from the outer perimeter fence, and he told him something much more important. Before he left on the night of his defection, he had placed several strips of duct tape over the latch on the door. He had made sure it was closed, but not locked. It would provide an easy access to the bomb shelter, and through it to the rest of the compound. All they had to do was figure a way to get through the fence undetected. Javan came up with a solution so simple that Don couldn't figure out why he hadn't thought of it himself. They would simply bypass it. Electrically, at least. With shielded cables, they would clamp the fence for a narrow section and then, with rubber gloves and rubber boots to prevent grounding themselves, they could cut a small opening to pass through single file. Death was coming our way. They would kill us all, and with the blessing of their Ayatollah, they would do it at night on their holy day. We would all die on a Friday.

So, just after full dark on a Friday evening in late August, the attack commenced. The clamps were placed, and a hole was cut in the fence where Don figured there was a partial blind spot in the CCTV system. Twenty-five fully armed Iranians, led by Don Davis, climbed through the hole and followed him single file to the escape tunnel entrance. As he promised, the door was not latched and opened with ease. In only a couple of moments the attack force was inside the compound.

They traveled the entire three-hundred-foot length of the escape tunnel, and Don was the first one through the door into the bomb shelter proper. He proceeded to the radio room and found Mike and Pat McCardle sitting at the shortwave radio wearing headsets as they monitored the frequencies, listening for any radio traffic from other Event survivors. Don raised his AK-47 and fired a long burst into their backs, killing them instantly, and destroying the radio in the process. The noise brought Phil and Doris Gardner rushing into the main room of the shelter and they were instantly gunned down by Afshin Javan, who was leading the raid, with Don Davis as his guide. In less than a minute, four of the Water Lily Warriors had been murdered, two by our own version of Norway's Vidkun Quisling, who had betrayed his countrymen to the Nazis during World War Two. Fortunately, there were no other people in the shelter. The others were all at the main house, having a glass of wine as our designated chefs, including my wife Dottie, prepared the evening meal.

Due to the soundproof qualities of the bomb shelter no one, including the people enjoying their wine on the screened porch, heard the shots fired that had killed four of their friends. Don Davis, followed closely by Javan, ran to the main house front door and the others fanned out around the compound grounds with orders to kill all who exited the main house when the shooting started. I was helping to set the dining room table when I heard Dottie scream. I ran to the kitchen to find, to my horror, Don Davis holding her from behind, with a butcher knife at her throat. Javan stood to one side watching what was about to happen.

With a big smile on his face, Don snarled "You killed the love of my life, and now I'm going to do the same to yours!" Out of instinct, I raised my left hand over my head. When Don involuntarily glanced up at my hand, I drew the Sig Sauer pistol from my holster and calmly shot him in the forehead. He dropped the knife and collapsed in a heap. I turned and fired three quick shots at the Iranian standing in the corner of the room in the "two to the body, one to the head" drill I practiced constantly. It was all over in seconds. The gunfire brought Ari and the others running into the room. The soundproof doors and windows hadn't alerted those on the porch however, or warned our attackers that they had been detected. I looked at the man who had accompanied Davis and was startled to see that he had bright blue eyes which were now lifelessly starring into eternity. Don, on the other hand, just looked surprised. My troubles with him were over. I walked over to Dottie, took her in my arms, and hugged her as she quietly sobbed against my chest. A tiny rivulet of blood trickled from a small cut on her throat. It had been that close.

Our ordeal was far from over, however. We had an unknown number of armed assailants in our compound.

How they got there undetected was a mystery, but they must be dealt with, and quickly. I ran to the front door and locked it, while Ari summoned those on the porch to get them out of harm's way. The way he did it was one of the bravest acts I have ever witnessed. Instead of shouting we were under attack, and thereby informing our attackers that they had been discovered, he casually walked among those on the porch and said that dinner was served. Everyone got up and filed into the house. They were all in great danger from automatic weapons that were surely pointed at them in the dark, but only Ari was aware of that fact, and still willingly exposed himself to save them. He was the last inside, and closed and locked the door behind him. We were now in a bullet proof building nearly as secure as the bomb shelter. But how could we get out? That was another question altogether.

The answer of course came from Bernhard Klaus. When I contacted him using the encrypted frequency on the house radio room shortwave set, he simply said "Move the center wine rack in the wine cellar." "There's another escape tunnel hidden behind it." Sure enough, when we attempted to move the rack, it slid forward with ease, even though it contained over five hundred bottles of wine. Behind it was another solid steel door which gave access to another tunnel. This one was over four hundred feet long, and its exit door was cleverly camouflaged under a large growing bush just past the tree line. When we left the exit in the darkness, we were invisible to the Iranian attack force, which had set up their positions within a hundred feet of the front and rear entrances to the main house.

There were eight of us, and we were all wearing night vision goggles from Bernhard's armory and carried automatic weapons, mostly the AK-47s we had obtained from the Iranians we killed on our patrols. We also carried fragmentation grenades which we had obtained in the same manner. By prearranged plan, Ari went to the left with Jack Swanson as his partner, and Dave Carson went right with Dan Lewis. I, along with my son Mike, his friend Kevin and Bill Fleming went down the middle and the Battle Royal commenced.

The next half hour was like nothing I had ever experienced before, or hope to again. The explosion of grenades, the sound of automatic weapons firing and bullets whizzing by my head. The shouts, the screams, it all blended into a cacophony of violence and death. A last shot was fired, and suddenly it was totally silent. All I could hear was the beating of my heart, my heavy breathing and the whistle of tinnitus which I had suffered with for years.

We had killed them all, but suffered only two casualties of our own. Kevin was shot in the thigh, but the bullet passed through without hitting bone or artery. Mike had applied pressure and covered the entry and exit holes with field dressings. Ari had been hit in the upper chest by shrapnel from a fragmentation grenade, but only a small piece had penetrated his flak vest and hit nothing vital at any rate. We summoned Janet and Peggy, and they immediately rendered first aid to our wounded while we checked the Iranians for signs of life. There were none. They were all dead. The adrenalin began to wear off, and I suddenly felt deathly tired. I could have fallen to the ground and slept for hours. But then a leader can't do that, can he?

Shortly after the shooting stopped the other members of our group began to appear out of the darkness to survey the destruction we had wrought. It was fearsome indeed. None of us, save Ari Zuckerman and Dave Carson, had seen carnage on this scale. Most of us had only seen a dead person at a church or funeral home memorial service prior to the Event, and the occurrences since then in Happy Valley. We had seen men killed on the way up here and had witnessed the murder of a friend, but none of that prepared us for tonight's horror. Twenty-five human beings destroyed in less than an hour. Little did we know that the total would shortly rise to twenty-nine.

We took a quick head count and discovered that the Gardner's and McCardle's were both missing. A short search discovered their bodies in the shelter. We were going to have four more funerals and burials to conduct tomorrow. We gathered up the dead Iranians and Don Davis, and placed their bodies under a large tarp until the morning, when they could be dealt with properly. As an afterthought Ari suggested that we place Don next to Charlene's grave. Not out of respect for the crazy bastard who had just tried to murder us all, but for Charlene, who had loved and guided him throughout decades of marriage together. They would now rest side by side on Bill's Mountain.

After a few hours of uneasy sleep, I got up, showered and went to the shelter kitchen to make a cup of coffee with the Keurig. As I walked through the main room, I passed the spot where the bodies of Phil and Doris Lewis had been discovered. The pool of blood had been covered by a sheet of black plastic until could be properly cleaned up this morning, but it still was a stark reminder of what had occurred. Four more of us killed by the same group of murderous thugs. "COEXIST!" Yeah, right.

The blood-spattered radio room where the McCardle's had been gunned down also had a sheet of the black plastic on the floor, in front of the now useless short-wave radios I used for my secure communications with Bernhard in Switzerland. The bullets which ended the lives of Mike and Pat had passed through them and shattered both sets. At that moment I said a silent prayer of thanks for the caution and forethought of Bernhard Klaus in being wise enough to duplicate the entire radio room setup in the main house basement. That's where I was headed next.

As I walked, I pondered our current situation. We are down to ten men capable of defending the group. Not to say that the women can't do that. They were all constantly armed while we were on our trek, but since arriving here at the Bill's Mountain compound they have assumed a more traditional role. Well, "traditional" for a bunch of seniors I guess I should say. Opposing us are an unknown number of radical Shia Iranian "Twelvers", well-armed and determined to wipe out all non-believers before the return of the Mahdi. This does not bode well for our survival, even in a compound as secure as this one. That was radically demonstrated by last night's raid.

When I got to the main house, I immediately went to the radio room. This was now our only lifeline to what remained of civilization after the Event. I contacted the Lausanne facility on an open frequency and asked to speak to Bernhard. I got the normal "Stand by" response. About ten minutes later, Bernhard came on and I told him to switch to the secure frequency. When contact was reestablished, I told him in detail what had occurred yesterday. Obviously concerned, he said "You will have to leave there, but first you must disrupt the plans of the Iranians." Then he said something which startled and confused me. "Have you ever flown a War Bird?" He said. A 'War Bird'? I thought. Did he mean like the World War Two vintage aircraft like the C-47 he had in the GSP hangar, or one of the fighters you used to see at airshows? "Well," I said "I have some stick time in T-6, T-28 and T-34 trainers, and I flew a highly modified P-51 for a cloud seeding experiment." "That will have to do." Said Bernhard. Fly down to GSP and take your son Mike with you. He's an A&P mechanic, right?" "Yes", I said, but why?" "Call on this frequency when you get there. I will have it monitored. Out". Well, that was cryptic, even for Bernhard. What did he have up his sleeve? I would soon find out, and it would be a real game changer!

Before I left for GSP we buried the Iranians in a mass grave that Bill Mason had dug with a bucket loader tractor. He then used the backhoe on the other end of the tractor to dig five more graves. Four in another area for the Gardner's and the McCardle's and one next to Charlene's grave for Don. Jack Swanson had to once again use his carpentry skills to build the coffins out of lumber in the barn. It was a combined funeral and burial service for the Gardner's and McCardle's, we didn't have the luxury of time to be more formal as was the case with Charlene. Nothing was said over the grave of our Quisling. He didn't deserve it. Again, the fact that we didn't dump his body in the mass grave with the Iranians was out of respect for Charlene's memory, nothing more.

CHAPTER XXIII

WHISTLING DEATH - THE CORSAIR SOLUTION

The trip to GSP took the standard 20 minutes, liftoff to touchdown. As always, I avoided the area of the Iranian compound. We taxied up to the Klaus hangar and did the standard procedure of pulling the Super Cub inside and closing the hangar door. I left the generator running and proceeded to the radio room, where I contacted Bernhard as requested. "Go to the main office and open the metal cabinet on the wall," He said. "There you will find a key with a red tag marked 'C'. It is to the smaller hangar next door. Go see what's in there and then call me in an hour. We have much to discuss. Out."

Another quick dismissal from Bernhard. He was putting me under pressure and he knew it, so this must be important. I found the key and Mike and I walked over the adjoining hangar. I unlocked and opened the door and we walked into the dimly lit hangar the only light coming from a couple of skylights on the roof. We were stunned with what we saw. There, ten feet in front of us, was an apparition from the past, a World War Two Vintage Chance-Vought F4U "Corsair", the airplane the Japanese called the "Whistling Death" because of the peculiar sound it made in a high-speed strafing run. The perfectly restored aircraft was painted in the original dark navy blue with white trim. Protruding from the leading edges of the wings were six .50 caliber machine guns. Its huge four bladed propeller marked it as a later model, which might have seen combat in Korea. Altogether it was an awesome sight to behold. As we slowly walked around the airplane, I noticed many wooden crates stacked against the back wall of the hangar. It turned out that they contained ammunition for the aircraft's armament. How had Bernhard been able to obtain that, I wondered? There was also a large drop tank attached to the belly of the plane. To extend its range as I remembered, then dropped when entering aerial combat.

The hour was nearly up, so I left Mike to examine the airplane further while I returned to the radio room and contacted Bernhard on the discrete frequency. "Could you fly that?" He asked. "Well yes, I probably could." I said. "But to what purpose?" "To strafe the Iranian compound and disrupt their operations, to give your group a chance to escape from Bill's Mountain before you are overwhelmed by those fanatics."

"The closest English-speaking destination in a "clear zone" I can come up with is Yarmouth, Nova Scotia, which is about nine hundred and fifty nautical miles away from the Bill's Mountain compound and well within range of the Dakota in my hangar at GSP." Bernhard said. "By my count there are only twenty-One of you left, including the children. The C-47 has the capability to fly non-stop all the way to Yarmouth, Nova Scotia with that load and full fuel tanks, maybe even to Halifax".

I told Bernhard that I'd have Mike give the Corsair a full going over, including fuel, oil and armament. Then we'd have to do the same with the C-47. The final piece of the puzzle was how to get the remainder of our group safely back to GSP. The entire route led through country nominally in control of the Iranian fanatics. I had an idea how that might be done, but kept it to myself until I had a chance to study that option.

I told Bernhard that I would contact him tomorrow at the normal time, and then signed off. Mike locked up the Corsair hangar, and after removing the Super Cub from the big hangar, we shut off the generator and left for the compound. As soon as I got there, I called for a group meeting that evening after dinner. We had a lot to discuss. Then Mike and I sat down to hash over what we had seen and done that morning. That's when Mike came up with a jewel of an idea. "I think I can turn that drop tank into a bomb." He said. "If we cram it with C-4 and top it off with diesel fuel, it will explode like napalm when it hits, as long as we include a couple of detonator caps on the C-4." "That would definitely get their attention!" I said. "Especially if I dropped it

on the roof of the mosque during their Friday prayer service."
"They'll get to meet their Twelfth Imam sooner than they
thought." I had made the transition. After what they had
already done to five of us, and planned to do to the rest, I no
longer thought of them as human beings, but rather vermin,
to be destroyed before they could destroy us.

Late that afternoon I took a short solo reconnaissance
flight. I knew what I was looking for, and shortly found it.
A one-mile long stretch of straight highway wide enough to
be a runway, and clear of obstructions on both sides. There it
was below me, on the opposite side of Bill's Mountain from
the Iranian compound. About a mile and a half walk down-
hill. The Water Lily Warriors could do that in their sleep, I
thought. I had a big smile on my face as I landed the Super
Cub. Things were at last headed in the right direction.

Everyone but our night guards were there at the meeting
in the media room. I explained in detail what I had discussed
with Bernhard, I told them about the Corsair, the armament
it carried, and that Mike thought we could make an effective
bomb out of the drop tank. This information was a bit much
for some of them to absorb, but most of the men understood
the concept, especially Ari and Dave Carson. Finally, I told
them that I wanted to make the raid on the Iranian compound on the following Friday and then fly the Corsair back
to where Mike would be waiting with the C-47. I would then
fly it to Bill's Mountain and land on the highway, loading up
the group and what belongings we were going to bring with
us and fly back to GSP to refuel and depart for Nova Scotia
the following morning. Piece of cake. Or at least I hoped so.

We now had five days to prepare for the attack on the Iranian compound and our departure.

The next morning Mike and I flew back to GSP. We carried twenty-five pounds of C-4 plastic explosive and several detonator caps. Today we would become bomb makers. When we entered the Corsair's hangar the first task was to load the .50 caliber ammunition for the planes machine guns. There was a complete set of maintenance manuals, an armorer's handbook and a pilot's flight training manual as well. Each gun would have four hundred rounds in its belt fed magazine, so with all six guns firing, that meant, twenty-four hundred rounds could be placed on a target. It was greatly feared by Japanese soldiers, and I was confident it would wreak havoc on the Iranian compound.

While Mike oiled and loaded the guns, I climbed up on the wing and got in the cockpit. The first thing that struck me was that it was going to be a bitch to taxi. The long cowling made forward visibility virtually nil on the ground. I would have to constantly "S-turn" to stay centered on the taxiways. With the eleven-thousand-foot-long runway at GSP, takeoff shouldn't be a problem. I'd line her up, lock the tailwheel, and accelerate gradually, not going to takeoff power until I got the tailwheel off the ground and could see straight ahead. I spent the next hour going through the pilot's flight training manual and familiarizing myself with the various switches and controls. This was

going to be a one-shot deal. Training flight and combat mission rolled into one, with a seventy-six-year-old student pilot at the controls.

I got out of the cockpit and helped Mike pull the massive four bladed prop through multiple revolutions to clear the engine of any hydraulic lock which might be there because the oil had pooled in the lower cylinders of the massive radial engine. After that, Mike checked the tire pressures and we turned our attention to the drop tank, which would become our makeshift bomb. Tapping on it, we determined if was empty. Good. Nothing to drain out and dispose of. Mike removed several access panels on the top of the tank and we proceeded to load the C-4 and detonators. Mike closed up the panels and we went back to the main hangar and began the laborious task of lugging diesel fuel in five-gallon cans, to hand fill the drop tank. We loaded one hundred gallons, enough to make a big fuel-air explosion when the C-4 detonated on impact.

It was late in the afternoon when we completed the work and flew back to Bill's Mountain. After dinner, I collapsed into a dreamless sleep and didn't wake up until eight the next morning. Unusual for me, but an indication of the stress I was under. I contacted Bernhard, and informed him of our plans, including the decision to leave for Nova Scotia this coming Saturday, after my attack on the Iranian compound on Friday. He said he had some valuable contacts in Halifax, and would let them know we were on the way.

I called another group meeting and we decided that we would reassemble the wheeled travois and use them to carry as much of the freeze-dried food packets as we could manage. My granddaughters would ride in ones pulled by Matt and Megan, and Kevin Landry in another, pulled by Dave Carson, as he was unable to walk any distance with his leg wound. Sleeping bags and extra ammunition would round out the loads. It was about a mile and a half down a narrow trail to the highway where I would land the C-47, so we couldn't make use of the ATVs. We determined that the next three nights would be a celebration of our survival thus far. The ladies would make gourmet meals with meats from the freezer, and we would consume the best of Bernhard's vintages. We would lock up when we left, and booby trap the area to discourage attempt at burglary by the Iranians who survived my attack.

There was one downer in all this. Obviously, we couldn't take the stallion and the mare. We would lead them down the mountain and release them outside the fenced and booby-trapped outer compound. Bill and Suzi loved these animals, but the hoped-for stud farm was just another casualty of the catastrophe which had devastated most of the planet.

Friday morning dawned bright and clear. It was going to be the last day on Earth for a lot of people. I just hoped I wasn't going to be one of them. I thought of the old saying about airline pilots. You don't know what's worse, walking out to the airplane knowing this is going to be your last flight, or walking out to the airplane **NOT** knowing this is your last flight. Graveyard humor, I guess! Mike and I had breakfast. Then I hugged my family, Dottie extra tight, and told everyone I'd see them down on the highway this afternoon. I dearly hoped I would. We climbed in the Super Cub and took off for GSP.

When we arrived, we used a tug to pull the C-47 to the front of the hangar so it could be easily removed in preparation for the flight to pick up the group from Bill's Mountain that afternoon. We then went over to the next hangar, open the doors, and pushed the Corsair onto the ramp. After closing the hangar doors, I got in the cockpit and with Mike standing by with a fire extinguisher, started the engine. We had once again pulled the prop through for ten blades. No sign of a hydraulic lock. When I hit the starter button the prop turned over easily and after counting eight blades, I turned the magneto switch to the both position. The engine immediately sprang to life, belching great clouds of white smoke and then settling down to a smooth idle. I let it run until the cylinder heat temperature gage began to rise, and then shut it down. I was ready to roll.

I planned to attack the mosque during the Dhuhur prayer which was at about one P.M. according to the information I had received from Bernhard, so I had about two hours to wait. We went back to the main hangar, opened the main hangar door, and started up the C-47. The hangar was now basically empty, and I didn't run the engines above idle, so nothing was disturbed. I shut the engines down. We were ready to go as soon as I returned from the raid, and we re-closed the hangar door. I found a set of flight coveralls that fit, and a helmet and parachute as well. As departure time approached, I put everything but the helmet on, gave Mike a big hug and climbed up on the gull winged fighter and into the cockpit. Mike helped me with the shoulder straps and I put on the helmet, blew him a kiss and he jumped off to again be my fire guard when I started the engine. I went through the before starting checklist, checked to see the parking brake was set, and started the engine, which again ran smoothly.

Mike pulled the wheel chocks, gave me a thumbs up and I saluted him and started my taxi.

As I had expected, it was a bear to taxi this long-nosed beast, but I successfully negotiated the procedure and lined up on the runway and locked the tailwheel. I did a run up and checked the mag switches. Everything was perfect. Could I expect anything less from something owned by Bernhard Klaus? It was now or never. I pushed up the throttle and started the takeoff roll. As I planned, I didn't give it too much power until I got the tail up and had forward visibility, then I slowly advanced the throttle to takeoff power. The airplane lifted off at something just over one hundred miles an hour. I saw a positive rate of climb, retracted the gear and flaps, and reduced to climb power. Whistling Death was on its way and an Imam was climbing a minaret to call the faithful to Dhuhur, their third prayer of the day. For many of them, including him, it would be their last.

Since it was just past noon there was no way I could approach the compound "out of the sun", so I elected to fly low up the valley, drop the "bomb" on the mosque and then reverse course, making as many strafing runs as I could until I ran out of ammo. I started far down the valley at an altitude of only a hundred feet or so and an indicated airspeed of three hundred and fifty knots. Maybe not balls to the wall, but I was sure I was "whistling" big time. I armed the machine guns and flipped the cover up on the drop tank release switch. I had only one chance at this, so I'd better make it right. I could now see the glimmer of the stark white mosque in the distance, I was closing on it rapidly. My right hand was on the joystick and my left on the drop tank switch.

Suddenly, as things appear to do in times of great stress, everything went into slow motion. I didn't see anything but the mosque with its four minarets and large round dome. When that nearly filled the windscreen, I pulled back on the stick and hit the switch. I felt the weight of the drop tank leave the airplane and suddenly I felt, rather than saw, a great explosion behind me. It had worked! By God it had worked! I glanced up at the rear-view mirror in the cockpit and all I could see was a giant ball of flame. I banked hard to the left, leveled the wings and flew straight for about a quarter mile and then banked hard right in a classic ninety/two-seventy reverse course maneuver. As I turned, I descended back to about fifty feet AGL to begin my strafing runs. The sight that greeted me as I completed the turn almost took my breath away.

The great dome of the mosque was totally engulfed in flames and two of the minarets were completely gone, toppled by the exploding C-4 and diesel fuel. I could now see people and vehicles on the ground. Some were running away from the mosque, a few with their clothes on fire. Others were headed towards it, perhaps in an attempt to rescue their comrades. I didn't care. I began firing the guns in short bursts. I could see the dirt being kicked up as the .50 caliber slugs hit the ground. I saw people falling under the hail of lead, and a truck explode as I hit its gas tank. It again felt like it was happening in slow motion. I continued making the ninety/two-seventy turns, making repeated strafing runs on the entire Iranian compound.

On the sixth such maneuver I heard and felt bullets hitting the airplane. The bastards were fighting back. I had to respect them for that. As I came back for another run, I felt more rounds hit the airplane and suddenly saw black smoke, followed by flames, erupt from the engine cowling. I was hit in a vital spot, and hit bad. I pulled up sharply, oriented myself, and headed back towards GSP. If I bailed out around here, I was a dead man. I spotted the airport dead ahead and pulled up to about two thousand feet AGL. That slowed me down to about two hundred knots, but the flames were getting worse. As I was coming up on the airport, I pointed the airplane towards open country to the south, rolled inverted, opened the canopy, released my seatbelt and shoulder harness, and dropped from the airplane. "Wow", I thought. "My first parachute jump!" It might be my last too.

CHAPTER XXIV

HEAVY METAL - THE HIGHWAY LANDING

As I dropped away from the airplane, I was falling face up, looking straight up at the burning Corsair. Common sense, and watching sky diving videos on YouTube, told me this wasn't the right position to open a parachute. I spread my arms and legs wide, and with a little experimenting was able to roll face down. I then pulled the "D-ring" and felt the drogue shoot come out, followed by the pleasant shock of the parachute deploying above me. I grabbed the right riser, and was able to turn slowly around till I could see the airport coming up below me and the smoke and flame of where the Corsair had crashed in what appeared to be an open field several miles away. I was descending towards a grassy area between the taxiway and the runway. The grass was quite high, not having been mowed for over a year, so it cushioned my landing. I remembered to bend my knees before touching down, so although it wasn't smooth, it wasn't that bad, either, kind of like jumping off a six-foot wall into a hayfield.

I stood up to see Mike running towards me. "Are you alright Dad?" He said as he got nearer. "Yes." I replied. "I guess this qualifies me for membership in the Caterpillar Club!" "What's that?" He asked as he helped gather up the chute while I got out of the harness. "It's an organization of people whose lives have been saved by a parachute after they jumped from a crippled airplane." I explained. "For sure dad, for sure. What happened?"

"Well, the mosque is no more." I said. "I don't know how many people were in there when I dropped your bomb, but I'm pretty sure there were very few who survived. The explosion was enormous." "When did you get hit?" Mike asked. "On my sixth and seventh strafing runs." I said. The last rounds must have hit a fuel line or something. The smoke and fire were almost instantaneous, but the engine kept running, thank God. If I had to bail out there, I would have been red meat for those guys. I stirred up a real hornet's nest!" "I think I bought us some time, they won't go on the offensive until they've licked their wounds and buried their dead."

We walked back to the Klaus hangar, and I got on the radio to give Bernhard an update on what had happened. "I'm sorry I lost the Corsair. "I said. "But it did a helluva a lot of damage before they made that lucky hit.". "It was expendable." Bernhard said, "It's kind of poetic that the old warbird would meet its end fighting to save American lives. I'm proud of you, old boy!" "Well thanks." I said. "Now its time for my next trick, landing the C-47 on a state highway!" "A what?

What are you talking about?" Asked Bernhard. I proceed to tell him the entire plan, and that we would be leaving shortly to pick up the survivors on the highway just north of the Bill's Mountain compound. "It's the best and safest way to get them out of there." I said. "Trying to get around the Iranians on the ground would just be too dangerous and time consuming." "I will of course have to leave that up to you." He said. "But for God's sake be careful."

Assuring him I would, I signed off, and Mike and I, with the help of a small diesel tug, pulled the C-47 out of the hangar and into the brilliant sunlight. Mike closed the hangar door while I did the before starting checklist. I heard the cabin door being closed, and soon Mike came forward and sat in the right seat. We started the engines and taxied out to begin our rescue mission. A long and exciting day was about to get longer. Reaching the end of the runway, I taxied into position, locked the tailwheel, and began the takeoff roll.

I turned due west after takeoff. I had flown a DC-3 many years ago, and the memories began to transition from my brain to my hands. Compared to a modern airliner with hydraulic boosted flight controls, this venerable old aircraft felt heavy. However, as I made a few "S-turns" to get the feel of the C-47, I realized that this could be a virtue, not allowing the pilot to be sloppy and over-control the airplane on approach and landing. Since this landing was going to be on a highway that was maybe 50 feet wide at best, I had to be precise, and keep her in the middle of the road.

After telling Mike what I had in mind, I lowered the landing gear and selected full flaps. I wanted to feel what she felt like in this configuration. I then slowed to just above stall speed and flew in that "slow flight" mode for several miles before retracting the gear and flaps and heading towards Lake Lure and Bill's Mountain. Descending to landing pattern altitude, I spotted my chosen piece of state highway and flew along its length. Sure enough, there at the backside of Bill's Mountain, all standing in a hayfield together, were the survivors of our group. Out on the road itself was Ari, holding the makeshift wind sock in his hand. It was indicating a breeze blowing almost directly down the highway, and away from the group. Perfect!

I reversed course and set up on a left downwind landing pattern. I would ideally land about five hundred feet down from my selected runway length and then roll out directly in front of the group and make a quick one hundred and eighty degree turn on the road in preparation for loading and takeoff if there wasn't too much tailwind. As I passed abeam of the imaginary end of my runway, I called "Gear down, full flaps", and Mike complied. I eased the throttles back and called for the landing final checklist. That completed, I turned base and then final, descending at a normal rate and concentrating on my touchdown target. "Please Lord, don't let me screw this up" I thought in a silent prayer.

At five hundred feet AGL the highway looked as narrow as a sidewalk. I focused on staying right on the center of the dotted yellow line. At about ten feet above touchdown I flared slightly and eased the power back to just above idle. For safety, this would be a "wheel Landing" giving me the best forward visibility in this ancient tail-dragger aircraft. We touched down, bounced slightly, and then settled onto the highway as I closed the throttles. I slowly lowered the tail, and was down to taxi speed a thousand feet prior to reaching the group, who were now waving their arms and cheering the old "War Bird" who would take them to safety. "Good job Papa!" As my granddaughter Vicky would say. I did my one-eighty turn on the road and parked the brakes, shutting down the engines.

As I did the secure cockpit checklist, Mike got up and went back to open the cabin door. Ari came up, congratulated me on the landing, and asked how I wanted everything loaded. After the war, the C-47 had been converted to civilian use. It now had a small closet and a restroom just aft of the cockpit, and twelve rows of seats, one on either side. Only four windows, two per side, were left uncovered when it was re-converted to war bird status and painted in the D-Day paint scheme, olive drab, with black and white "Victory Stripes" on the inboard section of the wings to discourage "friendly fire" from overanxious anti-aircraft batteries on ship and the beaches at Normandy.

I told Ari to load all the freeze-dried food packets in the front seats as well as the weapons and ammunition we were taking along for safety. The men would sit in the forward seats, and the women and children in the back, for better load distribution. I got up and went out to do a walk-around inspection. There, I witnessed a sad sight. Bill and Suzi Mason were saying goodbye to their beloved horses, accompanied by Matt, Megan and our granddaughters. It was a tearful occasion, everyone but two-year-old Faye was crying, and she was hugging a front leg of the mare, saying "Up, up!" The horses would now be left to procreate on their own, not on the stud farm the Masons had envisioned. I wondered if all the abandoned horses would eventually form herds of "Mustangs" like those created when the Spaniards left portions of the Southwest in the seventeen hundreds. It was a nice thought, at least.

I gently cut short the process, telling everyone they must get aboard so we could depart this potentially dangerous area. When everyone was loaded, and I was about to close the door, I heard a sound, and saw a sight which chilled me to the bone. Coming down the road, about two miles away, were three ATVs. The Iranians were coming, and it wasn't to say goodbye!

I closed the door, ran to the cockpit and began starting the engines. We had no time to lose. Death was right behind us! As soon as the second engine started, I selected takeoff flaps, released the brakes, and applied takeoff power. They couldn't be more than a mile away now, maybe closer. I got the tail up and we began accelerating. We were now much faster than the ATVs, but not faster than a bullet from an AK-47! As I reached takeoff speed, I lifted off, climbed to about fifty feet AGL and then leveled out, retracted the landing gear and flaps, and continued to accelerate. Speed was life at that moment, and we were a poorer target low to the ground and getting faster all the time. I flew just above treetop level until we were over Lake Lure. With Rumbling Bald Mountain on our right and Chimney Rock straight ahead, we started our climb. I could hear cheering from the back. We made it!

The flight back to GSP was uneventful. We landed there about twenty minutes after our takeoff from the highway and taxied to the Klaus hangar. After I shut down the engines, everyone deplaned and the hangar door was opened so the

C-47 could be towed inside and prepared for tomorrow's flight to Nova Scotia. Much needed to be done, but first we mounted a double guard around the hangar, and a spotter on the roof with binoculars and a scope mounted rifle. We hadn't seen any sign of Iranians around the airport in the past, but they had to have figured where the C-47 had come from. I wanted the airplane fully fueled and prepared for takeoff on a moment's notice should the need arise. I was amazed they had arrived at Bill's Mountain to threaten our takeoff so soon after the raid on their compound with the Corsair. Perhaps that had been a patrol which was absent from their compound when my attack commenced, and they had been notified of that action by radio. With that thought in mind, I had the Super Cub taken from the big hangar and placed in the hangar which had housed the Corsair. I might want to do one last reconnaissance flight before we left.

CHAPTER XXV

DEFIANCE

As the others prepared for a good night's sleep or a rapid departure, I went over to Matt and Megan and asked them if they'd like to take a short flight with me to have a last look at where they'd spent the last five years of their life. They agreed, and left the girls with Ari's wife Rachael.

We all walked over to the hangar next door and pulled out the Super Cub. It was really only meant for two people, sitting in tandem, but Matt could push the rear seat back and allow Megan to basically sit on his lap. When I got them secured, I got in the front seat and started the engine. Since the wind was calm, I elected to takeoff to the south, which would pass just east of their old neighborhood. Once airborne, I climbed to five hundred feet AGL and turned slightly right so we would pass directly over their house.

Again, the devastation below was shocking. It seemed that every other house was a burned-out shell, and there were no signs of life anywhere. Could all these people be dead, or had at least some of them escaped, but to where? Now just below us was their house. I descended a couple of hundred feet and showed them how we had discovered the message they had scrawled on the garage door with black paint. They didn't have binoculars, and I didn't want to go any lower, but the writing was plainly there. "The Cabin in The Woods!" It said, and that led us to find them safe at the Klaus compound on Bill's Mountain.

Since we had plenty of daylight left, I decided to take the short flight to Bernhard's place. I stayed well south of the Iranian compound, and approached Bill's Mountain from the south, passing over Lake Lure in the process. I marveled at the improvised "runway" I had used to rescue the group this morning. It really looked short from here. Were the Iranians I had spotted in the three ATVs still around, or had they gone back to their compound? There was no way of knowing, so I stayed several thousand feet up, rather than chance being hit by a lucky shot from an AK-47.

I slowly circled the mountain. Everything looked tranquil below. That's when I saw them. The stallion and the mare had returned to the paddock where they had been kept since our caravan arrived months before. It had become their home, so when Bill and Suzi had been forced to abandon them, they made their way back to that small spot which meant security to them. I descended a few hundred feet for a better look, and the stallion suddenly rose onto his back legs in the classic fighting stance we've all seen in the movies. It was as if he was saying "We'll be alright. I'll take care of her." I was touched, Megan and Matt as well.

I turned back to depart the area the same way I approached it and suddenly spotted something that had not been there on our departure in the C-47 earlier in the day. There, on the tall flagpole atop Chimney Rock, was a large American flag. As we got closer, I realized there were hundreds of people on the rock, many waving smaller versions of the flag or simply waving their arms at us. So, there were other survivors of the event, and here, high in the Blue Ridge Mountains, was where some of them had gone. I felt a lump in my throat as I circled the area, wagged the Super Cub's wings in salute, and then departed to the east towards GSP. Even though we were soon leaving for Nova Scotia, there was still something to return to.

As I began my descent for landing, movement on the ground to the north caught my eye. I turned in that direction for a closer look. What I saw sent a chill down my spine. It was a column of ATVs, maybe thirty of them, and they were all headed for GSP. They were only about fifteen miles away, less if they went cross country. We had to leave, and fast. I had a walkie-talkie, so I called Ari and advised him of the approaching danger. I told him to pull the C-47 out of the hangar, get everyone aboard and then close the hangar door, turn off the generator and lock everything up. We were on the ground in five minutes.

I taxied up to the Corsair hangar and we jumped out, pushed the Super Cub into the hangar, and closed and locked the hangar doors. A rapid check showed everyone on board. I did a quick preflight check and got in the airplane, closing the door behind me. Mike already had the right engine running, and he started the left one as I taxied to the end of the runway for a takeoff to the south, away from the oncoming Iranians. I knew we were at maximum takeoff weight, possible slightly above, so I wanted all of that runway available for takeoff and initial climb out. I taxied onto the runway, told everyone to hang on, and pushed the throttles up to takeoff power. The airplane accelerated slowly. I got the tail up at about thirty knots and finally lifted off after what seemed an eternity, at least twice the normal takeoff roll, I imagined. I climbed out straight ahead for about five miles, not turning northeast until I was confident that I was well clear of any danger from our pursuers. I pulled out my charts and took up the desired course. Halifax, here we come!

As we climbed higher, away from the setting sun, my thoughts went back to those people high on Chimney Rock. They were surely in an easily defended area if they had the weapons to do so. I imagined they had, or they wouldn't be there, one year after the Event, and so close to the peril of being slaughtered by the Iranian "Twelvers". I only wished that there had been some way to communicate with them. Perhaps that would come later. For now, they, like us, must take care of themselves, and have faith that their country would rise like a Phoenix from the ashes of the event which was inflicted by our mortal enemies and the forces of nature.

Now, the survivors of the Water Lily Warriors were headed into the unknown, flying at night, over water, in a seventy-five-year-old airplane being flown by a seventy-six-year-old pilot. Unbelievable, but then that could accurately describe the events we had experienced over the last year and a half, truly unbelievable. The world may not have come to an end, but for a very large segment of the population, their lives indeed had. What would happen to us in Nova Scotia? Would we be welcomed as refugees, or reviled as invaders? Only time would tell.

All those thoughts passed through my mind as darkness fell and I detoured around a line of thunderstorms ahead. Heavy rain began beating on the skin of the aircraft, and brilliant lightning flashed around us while claps of thunder could be heard over the sound of the engines. Thankfully, we broke into the clear just before we departed the coast of Virginia, on the long over ocean part of our journey.

It's an old piston pilot's joke that when you get over the water the engines start running rough, and when nightfall occurs, they get REALLY rough! I just hoped that this old girl had one last long flight in her, or our story would end here, in the cold waters of the North Atlantic Ocean.

CHAPTER XXVI

INTO THE DARKNESS

A year and a half ago, only a few months prior to the event which had turned our lives into chaos, I had flown as a passenger on a flight from Charlotte to Madrid, Spain. As a retired pilot, I rarely got a chance to ride in First Class anymore. Those desirable seats almost always went to upgrading full fare passengers. That night, however I was lucky. I got the last First-Class seat, which was located on the left side of the airplane. As a result, I got a chance to view a sight which was very familiar after my long career as an international airline pilot. Most people think that a flight to Europe from the East Coast of America immediately departs over the ocean. In fact, since airplanes follow a "great circle" route to Europe, you hug the coastline on the way to your "coast out" point, which is generally in Newfoundland, anywhere from St. Johns to Gander. So, for several hours on a clear night you view the lights of a myriad of cities along the coastline of the Northeast U.S. and the Canadian Maritime Province's. That was so before the Event. Tonight, as the sun set in the west, it quickly became totally black. It was a moonless night and there was a high overcast, blocking any view of the stars above.

I had a six or seven-hour flight ahead of me, and it was going to be all "dead reckoning". There were of course no ground-based navigation aids, and I couldn't even do a rudimentary celestial check with no stars in view. Now I could better understand what the old Pan American Clipper pilots experienced in the 1930s, except they had four engines, tons of fuel, and indeed were flying seaplanes, which could land in the water if it wasn't too rough down there.

The C-47 droned on into the darkness. At our altitude of ten thousand feet MSL, I would have been able to see many lights along the shore of the Eastern seaboard a year and a half ago. Tonight, nothing was visible. It was as black as if we were flying in a bowl of squid ink. Years of flying techniques reemerged from my subconscious. I constantly made small adjustments to the elevator trim wheel. People must be moving around back there, I thought. Mike had fallen asleep in the right seat. It had been a long and trying day for all of us. For some reason I thought of a line from a poem by Robert Frost. "But I have promises to keep, and miles to go before I sleep......." That was surely the case for me on this ink black night over water. I had promised the people in the back, my wife, children and grandchildren included, that I would get them to safety in Nova Scotia if I had to tie a rope to the nose of this old airplane and drag it there. I was exhausted, but had many miles to go before I would be able to sleep.

The cockpit door opened, and Ari stuck his head in and said: "Coffee?" "You read my mind." I replied. I shook Mike and told him to go back and get some real shut-eye. I would need him awake and alert as we approached Yarmouth, roughly six hours from now if my calculations were correct. I dearly wished that this old bird had an auto-pilot, but it didn't. Mike had taken a few flying lessons when he was in his teens, but never soloed, let alone got a pilot's license. He could keep it straight and level in VFR conditions, when he had a horizon for reference, but he was no good on instruments, as I discovered when I let him handle the controls for a bit after it got fully dark. Instrument flying was an acquired skill, mastered only after hours of practice.

Ari soon returned with a steaming mug of instant coffee, heavily laced with sugar, to help keep me awake. He climbed into the right seat vacated by Mike, and handed me a packet of cookies from one of the pre-packaged MREs that were part of the larder at the Bills Mountain compound. I happily munched on them as Ari started a conversation obviously intended to keep me awake. "Dark as hell out there!" He said. "Yeah" I said. "There's no moon, and we wouldn't see it if there was. There's a solid overcast above us." Out of habit, I looked at the chart and flight plan on my lap-board. "I figure we've got about six hours or so left before we make landfall in Nova Scotia." I said. "I never got a chance to ask Bernhard if they still had navaids and VHF communication capabilities up there. I was going to give him one last call on the shortwave, but our rapid departure made that impossible."

"I would guess they still do if they have power up there, which apparently is the case." He said. "Well, that would be a blessing." I commented. "I am doing this strictly on dead reckoning, flying a plotted compass course and just guessing at the winds aloft. If we have too much crosswind from the west, we could end up flying past Nova Scotia without ever seeing it. That would be the end for all of us." "I understand." He said. "Realistically, what's the chance of that happening?" "Well, I plotted a track which would take us farther inland than I'd like, because we don't have enough fuel for a large deviation." I said. "Hopefully we'll be able to spot the coastline at first light and make corrections based on that. If they do have an NDB or better yet a functional VOR at Yarmouth, we can cut miles off the flight. Keep your fingers crossed." "Unfortunately, I don't have aeronautical charts for Canada, but we can start slowly scanning the NDB frequencies to see if somethings comes in. With luck, at this altitude we could pick up a bounce wave signal over five hundred miles out. Not enough for accurate navigation, but at least giving us an idea if we are way off course. We can start that in about a half hour from now."

We did. I showed Ari how to turn on the ADF receiver and rotate the dial slowly through the most likely frequencies. If by chance there was still an AM radio station broadcasting on Nova Scotia, we could even home in on that. It wasn't a particularly accurate form of radio navigation, but could at least confirm whether we were grossly off course, and point us in the right direction.

An hour went by. Then two. Suddenly, Ari exclaimed "I think I've got something!" I grabbed my headset and turned up the volume control. Faintly, but readable, I could hear Morris Code. "QI....QI....QI". I remembered from some lost bit of data that my brain had stored from all those years flying international routes out of JFK that the Field Identifier for the Yarmouth Airport, one of our "Rim Alternates" on the North Atlantic routes, was CYQI. "THAT" S IT!" I shouted. "That's the Yarmouth NDB!" I then selected the ADF position on the selector switch and watched as the pointer on the ADF indicator slowly swung around. It settled just slightly to the right of straight ahead. We were on course, and would probably be able to talk to the control tower at Yarmouth when we got closer. If they had an operating NDB, they surely were equipped for VHF communication as well, and Bernhard had told them we were coming. Hopefully, they would have someone monitoring the radio. I had never heard a sweeter sound in my life. We were going to make it. The Water Lily Warriors were going to survive. We had been airborne for nearly six hours, and I had planned for an average long-range cruise speed of about one hundred and thirty-five mph. I didn't know if we had a headwind or a tailwind affecting that speed. If the winds aloft were calm, we had about two hours remaining to Yarmouth, less with a tailwind, more with a headwind. I figured that at our altitude we would be able to make radio contact about a half hour out. That would be just about sunrise this time of year.

Then, off to the right, I noticed a glow in the pitch-black darkness. Could the sun be coming up already? No, not possible. Ari looked over his right shoulder and said: "Oh my God! It's on fire! The right engine is on fire!" The Grim Reaper had returned.

I pulled the throttle back and feathered the engine. Then I pulled the mixture to zero and turned off the fuel selector to the right engine. Thankfully, Ari soon said "It's out. The fire is out!" That's good, I thought, but we're still a long way out. Can we make it on one engine? The answer was no. Not at our weight.

Mike was there just after the fire went out. "That scared the crap out of everyone dad." He said. "Are were going to be all right?" "Not if we don't lose a lot of weight." I replied. "And fast!" "First, tie a rope around your waist and a helper for safety. Secure them to a seat by the main cabin door. Then wedge the door open and start throwing everything that's not bolted down out." "Start with the weapons and ammo, we won't need them if we make it to Nova Scotia, and they won't do us any good if we hit the water." "Next the food, and most of the water, sleeping bags and extra clothes. Like I said, anything that's not bolted down. If you've got any tools, start removing the seats, they can go too. We've got to be as light as possible if we have a chance of making it to land." "Okay," he said. "I'll get Dave to help me."

I explained my emergency plan to Ari. I started a gradual drift down towards the water, gaining speed and distance at the expense of altitude. It was standard procedure in an emergency of this type. I told him to select the international emergency frequency on the VHF radio and start putting out a "Mayday" call every minute or so, until hopefully we were in range of Yarmouth. It was all we could do. I slowed to a safe descent speed of a hundred knots and kept that as the altimeter slowly unwound from our cruising altitude of ten thousand feet towards the surface of the ocean, somewhere in the darkness below us. I said another silent prayer. "Please God, don't let it end here, so close to a safe harbor." I sure hoped He was listening.

Shortly, I heard the door open and the rush of air as someone, probably Mike, blocked the door open while the items I had described were jettisoned. I was descending at three hundred feet per minute, the least I could maintain while still holding a hundred knots with the remaining engine at a normal cruise power setting. At that rate, it would take over thirty minutes to get close to sea level, and we would be at least fifty miles closer to land. It would then be about six thirty, and that should be around first light at this latitude. I desperately needed to be in visual conditions, because I was going to fly down into what is known as "Ground Effect". We would be skimming just above the waves, and I couldn't trust my altimeter because I didn't know the correct barometric pressure setting for the area. The added aerodynamic buoyancy provided by ground effect could extend our range on the single engine we had left. It was basically our last hope.

Mike came forward and said "It's all out dad, except the seats. They're bolted down, and I only have one small crescent wrench to remove the bolts. It's a slow process." "I understand." I replied "Keep trying. Remove the ones forward and aft of the wing. Keep the ones over the wing for Suzi and the children. The rest of you will have to sit on the floor. Rig some rope to hang onto if there's any left back there." "Will do dad." He said, and he squeezed my shoulder in encouragement as he left.

Slowly, agonizingly slowly, the visibility began to improve. Dawn was coming, and not a second too soon. I could see we were now descending through thin layers of cloud. I hoped they would not continue all the way to the surface. I had to be in VFR conditions close to the water. At about two thousand feet we broke out of the last cloud layer and it was just bright enough to make out the waves below us. Not calm conditions for sure, maybe four to six-foot waves with some whitecaps. From their direction, I knew we had a headwind. Damn! We didn't need that too!

It would take us another six or seven minutes to descend into ground effect. I told Ari to make the mayday calls every thirty seconds from here on out. Was anybody listening? I had my headset volume turned way up when a response to our mayday came through loud and clear. "Roger Douglas Four-Seven Bravo Kilo, we read you weak but clear. What is your position and state your emergency?" I grabbed my microphone and answered. "We are unsure of our exact position, but on a track southwest of the Yarmouth NDB on a bearing of one hundred and thirty degrees to the beacon. We are on one engine, and descending into ground effect, over." "Roger Bravo Kilo, continue to transmit and we'll try to triangulate your position." Came the reply.

I told Ari to start repeating the phonetic alphabet so they could use radio detection finders to locate us. In about a minute we heard "Four-Seven Bravo Kilo", we have you on a track direct to the Yarmouth NDB, range seven zero, repeat seven zero nautical miles. Can you make it that far on one engine?" "We're damn well going to try!" I said. "We haven't come all this way to give up now!" "Roger that Bravo Kilo. We have alerted the harbormaster, and he is sending a launch in your direction just in case. This is Inspector Walsh of the

RCMP - better known as the Mounties to you folks south of our border. Welcome to Nova Scotia, and good luck."

I continued the descent towards the ocean, leveling out as low as I dared, perhaps less than ten feet above the highest waves. Wind driven spray splattered on the windshield as I cautiously advanced the throttle on the left engine to maintain at, or slightly above one hundred knots indicated airspeed. With concern, I saw the cylinder head temperature slowly start to rise towards the red line. If it over-temped and caught fire, we were basically all dead. A successful ditching in these conditions was virtually impossible. "Come on old girl!" I said out loud. "Just another half hour and we're home free."

The concentration required to maintain this altitude so close to the water was enormous, and I was exhausted. The adrenalin bursts were wearing me down, but I couldn't give up, for the sake of my loved ones in the back if nothing else. Then I saw it. A white Canadian Coast Guard launch dead ahead, and beyond it the coastline of Nova Scotia, brilliantly illuminated by the rising sun.

I gingerly climbed to five hundred feet. I dared go no higher on the single engine. At that altitude I proceeded to Yarmouth and when I had the airport in sight declared an emergency and proceeded directly to the airport. Since I feared causing any additional drag by extending any flaps, I only extended the landing gear, and that on a short final, when I knew we could glide to the runway even if the remaining engine failed. The landing was accomplished in that manner without further incident. The cheers from the back were deafening. A Jeep with a "Follow Me" sign on the back met us as I cleared the runway, and I indeed followed it to a parking spot on the ramp in front of a large hangar. I shut down the engine, and leaned over and kissed the left engine's throttle. That Pratt & Whitney R-1830 radial engine had saved our lives.

I looked up to see Ari staring at me and shaking his head. He slowly broke out in a big grin and made the Sign of the Cross with his right hand. "Thanks rabbi." I said. "We made it, didn't we?" He had to help me out of my seat. My legs felt like rubber. When I stepped out of the cockpit everyone was standing there looking at me. Most had tears in their eyes. Dottie stepped forward and gave me a big hug and a kiss. "You did it, Flyboy, you did it!" She said. "Let's go say hello to Canada." We walked arm in arm through our little band of survivors and I opened the cabin door and stepped out into the brilliant Canadian sunshine. Words cannot express how exhilarated and exhausted I felt, simultaneously.

I walked down the aircraft steps and stood on the ground looking at our welcoming committee. There were several individuals who I assumed were law enforcement personnel because of their uniforms. The rest were civilians. A tall uniformed gentleman stepped forward with his hand extended. "Inspector Walsh - RCMP". He said. "Helluva job Captain Farragut, one helluva job!" Next in line was a middle-aged man with thinning hair and thick lensed glasses. He shook my hand. "John Lawrence, Halifax representative for Bernhard Klaus. I concur with Inspector Walsh, a remarkable achievement. I have followed your exploits since your group first arrived at Bill's Mountain, but the long flight in this ancient aircraft must rank at the top!" He said. "I advised Mr. Klaus by shortwave as soon as we heard that your arrival was imminent. You must contact him as soon as you are rested. I will let him know that you're safely down. I have set up transportation to the Klaus compound outside Halifax for your group. We will leave as soon as your arrival details are settled with Inspector Walsh and the other Canadian authorities." "Thank you both for the kind words." I said. "Is Bernhard well?" "He is indeed, and wishes to talk to you using the normal communications procedures you established at Bill's Mountain. You'll be able to do that when we reach the Halifax compound." He replied. More of Bernhard's secrecy, but I had gotten used to that over the last few months. What was on his mind? I would discover that when we were conversing on the scrambled shortwave transmitters, but not before.

We didn't have much to unload from the airplane before it was towed into the hangar. Just a few articles of clothing and diapers for Faye. Everything else had been jettisoned over the Atlantic Ocean. I affectionately patted the C-47 on the left engine. I hoped she would be repaired and fly again. She had truly been our savior on that long over-water flight.

After the arrival formalities had been completed, we all boarded a large comfortable tour bus for the three-hour drive from Yarmouth to Halifax. Soon after leaving the airport I fell sound asleep, and didn't wake up till Dottie shook my shoulder and told me we were entering Bernhard's Halifax compound. Like Bill's Mountain. It was accessed through a gate in a high chain link fence, which I assumed was electrified as well. It was at least a mile from the gate to the main house. As we approached it, I was astounded to see that it was a slightly larger version of the one in North Carolina. I guessed that it was similarly equipped and stocked with supplies. Did it have a bomb shelter? I wouldn't be surprised. Mr. Lawrence gave me the keys to the main house. "There are ten en-suite bedrooms and a fully stocked kitchen, bar and wine cellar" He said. "Make yourself comfortable, and call Bernhard when you are rested. The radio room is in the basement. We have perimeter security guards, but none in the compound itself. I know you can handle that task yourself. Everything you need is in the armory, which is also in the basement. Rest well, and I will be in touch by telephone in the morning." So began the next phase of our adventure.

CHAPTER XXVII

HALIFAX

After we got everyone inside the main house, I held a brief meeting. I explained what Mr. Lawrence had said, and told everyone that the couples should all choose a room. It didn't matter which, since he indicated they were all the same, with two queen sized beds and a large en-suite bath. That accomplished, we went down to the armory and I issued a side arm with ammunition to each adult. I explained that there were guards around the perimeter of the compound, but that we were responsible for our own security while here.

That may have sounded a bit weird in the context of a normal society, in normal times, but this was neither. It was comforting to be here in what appeared to be a safe environment, but after eighteen months of literally fighting for our lives, I had grown very cautious, not paranoid. Nova Scotia may have been blessed to be one of the few places on the planet untouched by the ravages of the Event, but over ninety percent of the rest of the world was not. Could a new series of CMEs destroy society here as well? I certainly hoped not, but recent history had imprinted on my brain the concept that you must at least try to be prepared for any eventuality, however extreme. Our planet had become a classic example of Darwin's "Survival of the Fittest" theories.

These tasks accomplished, I told everyone I was desperately in need of a few hours' sleep, and that I would see them at dinner. I did, but it was at dinner the following evening. When my head hit the pillow, I slept the dreamless sleep of the dead for over twenty-four hours. The events of the previous two days had taken their toll, and my seventy-six-year-old body needed to re-charge the batteries.

I awoke to the late afternoon sun streaming through the window, and found a note from Dottie on the other bed. "I'll wake you in time to get ready for dinner, my love. I don't want to be the wife of Rip Van Winkle!" It said. I smiled as I read it. After all we had been through in the last year and a half, she still had a sense of humor, thank God!

I took a long, luxurious, steaming shower, and after shaving and brushing my teeth using implements supplied by our ever-thoughtful host, began to search for some clothing. I had awoken naked as the day I was born, and didn't even remember disrobing prior to falling into bed. I found my clothes in the closet. Everything from my underwear to my socks were freshly laundered and delightfully clean smelling. Dottie's work, I imagined.

It was nearly five-thirty when I left our room on the second floor and descended to the main level. Following the sound of voices, I walked into the Great Room off the kitchen, to find everyone else already there, obviously enjoying a glass of wine and some hors d'oeuvres before dinner. Suddenly, I was ravenously hungry, and thankful for a brimming plate of the delicacies which Dottie gave me, along with a glass of white wine from Bernhard's wine cellar. I was welcomed by the group, including Vicky and Faye, who came running across the room, demanding a hug and kiss from "Papa"!

Our dinner was an unbelievable feast, all cooked by our gourmet chefs, which I assumed included Dottie, with ingredients supplied from the walk-in freezer in the basement, or a delivery of fresh fruits and vegetables delivered by truck from Halifax at the direction of Mr. Lawrence the previous day. After a non-denominational blessing of the food and attendees by Rabbi Ari, we were served thick slices of standing rib roast cooked to perfection, accompanied by mashed potatoes, Yorkshire Pudding and broccoli spears. Dessert was a very British favorite of Spotted Dick Pudding, served with steaming hot coffee. I have never eaten better in a five-star hotel!

After the meal was cleaned up, we all met once again in the Great Room to discuss what came next. I informed them of Bernhard's request that I contact him as soon as I was rested enough to have a coherent conversation. I told everyone I had no idea of what he had in mind, which was true. I would contact him by shortwave radio in the morning, midafternoon Swiss time. I promised I would keep them totally in the loop. Then, I asked Ari to speak to us about our miraculous delivery from all the nearly incomprehensible forces of evil we had faced over the last year and a half. He stood up and reached into his pocket for his Yarmulke, removing it and placing it on the back of his head. In this manner, he symbolically became not just our friend and companion, but once again our non-denominational spiritual adviser. He slowly looked at each of us, and then began to speak.

"In the last year and a half, we have all lived through things that none of us could have predicted. We have had our lives turned upside down. We have lost friends in waves of violence that only a few of us have ever experienced before. We have seen some of our neighbors die by their own hand. We have witnessed some of our companions murdered in awful ways, by those they didn't even know, let alone hate. We have seen one of our number turn against us in a manner which is almost incomprehensible to us. We can only charitably hope that he was driven insane by grief, and as such not responsible for his actions against us. We have lived through all that."

"But." He continued, "We have also seen what can be accomplished when good people come together to fight against unbelievable adversity and evil. When they work together towards a common goal of survival. We have seen that for every instance of evil doing, there can be a counterbalancing act of kindness or courage. We have seen our humanity laid bare, but we have SURVIVED TOGETHER......TOGETHER!" He raised his voice when he spoke those last three words, something we had rarely heard him do. "We have all contributed to our survival. Some more than others, but none of us shirked from their duties when they were called upon. However, one, above all others, has made our deliverance possible. We all know who. Captain Farragut, just "Al" to us. Has led us to two places of refuge. First, to Bill's Mountain, in North Carolina, and now here to Halifax, Nova Scotia. Though many times he must have wished he could throw off the mantle of authority and responsibility we thrust upon him, he never attempted to do so. He sometimes, seemingly by force of will alone, has pushed, pulled, implored and occasionally cajoled us into doing something that at least some of us felt we were incapable of accomplishing." He paused for a long moment, once again looking into the eyes of every Water Lily Warrior in the room. You could have heard a pin drop in the silence. Then he spoke once again. "But he never gave up, and he never let us do so either. So tonight, as we stand or sit, clean, warm and with full stomachs, in a place of comfort and safety where he brought us, I want to express my gratitude, both to Almighty God, and to His chosen instrument, Al Farragut, who has truly delivered us from evil. Now please join me in reciting the Lord's Prayer." Everyone rose, and we did so. When it was finished, Ari walked over, shook my hand, and gave me a rib threatening bear hug. He was followed by all the rest, lastly my beloved wife. She stood there with tears of pride in her eyes. I hoped I wasn't crying too. By mutual consent the evening ended shortly thereafter. I had a very important radio call to make early in the morning, and I had no idea of what to expect from Bernhard. When I found out what he had in mind, it was a real shocker!

I was up at six in the morning. After a shower and a shave, I dressed and went down to grab a cup of coffee from the Keurig machine before going to the radio room in the basement. When I took my seat in front of the signal scrambling shortwave unit, I turned it on to warm up, and then sipped my coffee while I flipped through the pages of the frequency binder. In a minute or so I put on the headset and selected a familiar frequency in Lausanne. My transmission was quickly answered with the standard "Stand by one." In about five minutes, Bernhard came on the line. "Hello Al." He said. "I am so glad you made it to Yarmouth. It was a very tense nine hours here until Mr. Lawrence informed us of your safe arrival. Is everyone okay?" "Yes." I replied. "We are all fine. But the last two and a half hours hours, after the right engine caught fire and I had to shut it down, were a bit hairy. It was a close-run thing." "It was indeed, but your skill and perseverance made it happen." "Is there anything you need right now?" Bernhard asked. "We literally got here with only the clothes on our backs." I said. "Everything else we had to jettison to remain airborne. We of course have washed what we have, but will need changes of clothing and winter gear, as the season changes here. Can we arrange a loan?" "Don't be ridiculous! I have told Mr. Lawrence to add the names of your group to all our store accounts in Nova Scotia, and they are numerous. The only problem might be limited choices. Only what remains of the stock in the stores and warehouses when the event occurred is available, but I am sure your clothing needs can be satisfied. In addition, you will be supplied with Canadian Drivers Licenses, and a small fleet of diesel four-wheel drive vehicles will be placed at the compound for your use. Apparently, there is ample fuel, both diesel and unleaded available.

As fate would have it, two Super-Tankers had just arrived in the Halifax harbor when the event occurred. All the storage tanks are filled, and can be replenished many times from the tankers, which have become floating tank farms for the Nova Scotians use. They have years of fuel available." "That's wonderful news. I would assume the tankers were mostly filled with crude oil from the Middle East, so you must have at least one oil refinery on the island." "Yes." He said. "The Dartmouth Refinery. It had ceased operations in 2013, but thankfully was not demolished. When the EMP and CME events occurred last year, the local authorities quickly initiated plans to reopen it."

"Enough former employees were still in the area, and with their expertise they were able to get it up and running within six months. It now has the capacity to supply all fuel needs, including jet fuel, for the Province and even its neighbors to the north, for years to come." "Food then must be the only other possible problem, and from what we gathered prior to leaving Bill's Mountain, between what is grown or raised on land, and what is harvested from the sea, Nova Scotians are in good shape." "They are." Bernhard replied. "The island can feed its entire population, and a good many more, but that number is finite, of course." "I understand, and on behalf of all the others, I again thank you for your benevolence and generosity." I said. "But what matter did you want to discuss that require the use of the scrambled transmitters?" That's when he dropped the bomb. "I want you to go back to North Carolina." He said. "Not alone, and not in the C-47 or anything like it. I'm coming to Halifax in my Gulfstream G-550. My pilots are obviously familiar with the Greenville-Spartanburg airport, but not the surrounding area, and the dangers it represents. I want you to be the co-pilot. We won't land, just make a reconnaissance flight and return to Halifax. The aircraft has the range capability for that flight plan distance and much more. I have specially modified the G-550 to allow it to be depressurized so we can parachute items, or even people, from the aircraft. The purpose of the first mission will be to establish communications with the survivors you saw on top of Chimney Rock. We have to reestablish American civilization, and that's as good a place to start as any." I was stunned. Go back? To the place I had narrowly escaped with my life and the lives of all the others? I didn't know what to say, and my silence was deafening. "I know this must be hard to comprehend after all you've been through. Ponder what I've said, and contact me again in the morning. Out."

Out? **OUT**? My God, would I ever be able to understand Bernhard Klaus? Possibly, but it would take some doing. I resolved to think about what he had said, and not tell anyone, including my wife, what he had proposed. Instead, I called Mr. Laurence and arranged a shopping spree for the Warriors. They had earned it.

The people of Nova Scotia are among the finest I have ever had the pleasure to meet. An example of that is what occurred on September 11, 2001. After the terrorist attacks on the World Trade Center and the Pentagon, and the aborted attack on the White House or Capitol Building when United flight 73 crashed in Pennsylvania after the passengers attempted to regain control of the aircraft from the hijackers, all U.S. Airspace was shut down. Flights in our country were required to land at the nearest suitable airport, and flights inbound for our country from elsewhere were denied entry and diverted to alternate airports. For those arriving from Europe, that meant Canadian airfields. Because of limited fuel onboard after crossing the North Atlantic, finding a suitable airport was crucial. The standard Canadian Maritime Province's alternates of Gander and St. John's, Newfoundland were soon filled to capacity. Most flights didn't have the range to reach interior airports like Montreal or Ottawa, so Halifax and Yarmouth, Nova Scotia became the last resort between safety and disaster. They came through, and BIG TIME. Arriving flights quickly filled every available space on the ramps, so later arrivals were parked on taxiways and even one of the two runways at the Halifax airport.

As fate would have it, my daughter Megan, a new USAir flight Attendant at the time, was inbound from London to Philadelphia that morning. We knew that, and were greatly relieved when she called us at our home in New Mexico to tell us that she was safe on the ground in Halifax. As it turned out, her crew got some of the last hotel rooms available in the city. The residents of Halifax quickly came to the rescue of the stranded passengers, opening spare bedrooms in their homes, and providing meals and services for the next week until U.S. airspace was once again reopened, and the airliners could continue their flights to their original destinations. Megan, like the other stranded crews and passengers never forgot the kindness of the people of Halifax. Now, nearly twenty years later, she was experiencing that once again.

The bus arrived around noon to take us into town for our clothes and personal item shopping. As it turned out, we were semi-celebrities. The news of our somewhat spectacular arrival having been spread, first by word of mouth, and later by the local radio and television stations on their news broadcast. As I said before, there had been a few refugees arriving on boats from Maine and New Brunswick, but never a group our size, and from so far away. Pictures of our arrival at Yarmouth had been captured on several cellphone cameras, with the landing of the C-47, one engine visibly shut down, the taxi to the ramp on the remaining engine, and our group deplaning with Matt, Megan and our granddaughters next to last, followed by Dottie and I. A closeup showed the smoke and fire damaged right engine cowling. We later viewed this footage on the big screen TV in the media room at the compound.

There were several men's and women's clothing stores in Halifax, including one at their West End Mall and a Bass Pro Shop, where we could get cold weather coats and waterproof boots for the coming winter season. As Bernhard had implied, the selection was a bit limited, but we all got everything we needed, at least a week's worth of clothing apiece, maybe more. At each stop, the word of our arrival preceded us, and small crowds of people greeted us with applause and words of welcome. After what we had experienced during the last year and a half, particularly the last few months, it all seem surreal. Safety and normalcy in a secure environment had, only a couple of days ago, seemed totally out of reach.

On the way back to the compound, Megan asked the bus driver to stop at the small hotel where she had stayed after landing in Halifax on 9/11. He did so, and we all got off to look around the neighborhood. As it turned out, several of the staff who worked there in September of 2001 were still employees of the hotel. Megan was warmly welcomed, and even shown photographs taken at the time, which were hung on one wall of the lobby, along with grateful letters sent by passengers and crews of flights who stayed there that fateful week. To her amazement, the letter of thanks she had written was among them, along with a group photo of her crew, taken on the morning they left.

The hotel manager insisted on serving us an afternoon tea service, with small sandwiches and pastries. He absolutely refused any payment, which was fortunate, because there wasn't a cent, Canadian or otherwise, among us. After an hour or so, we all re-boarded the bus, to waves and applause of the small crowd that had gathered while we were there. It was a fitting end to our shopping spree. On the way back to the compound I stood at the front of the bus and told everyone I wanted to hold a group meeting at five o'clock to discuss my conversation with Bernhard that morning as well as begin to make plans for our future, as best we could.

I started the meeting with a simple statement. "Klaus wants me to go back to North Carolina." The room was immediately in turmoil with shouts of "No way! Is he nuts?" Or versions of the same. I held up my hand, and when silence prevailed, I spoke again. I explained the plan that Bernhard had outlined in our brief conversation, that we would be using his modified corporate jet to supply radios, and so establish communications with, the people we saw on Chimney Rock. We wouldn't land. I said that we had been very lucky to escape with our lives and come to this place of safety, but that I felt we had an obligation to do whatever we could to assure that our fellow Americans had at least a chance to survive as well. There was an unknown factor here. What had happened to the world governments after the Event? Why hadn't they done anything to help the people they supposedly represented? I suspected that I knew the answer to that. They had simply been overwhelmed by the enormity of the crisis that descended on them.

I said that I was sure that around the planet small segments of governments remained, sequestered in bunkers like that which was rumored to exist beneath a resort hotel in West Virginia for members of Congress and other important government officials. Something similar was undoubtably in place at Camp David for the President and the rest of the Executive Branch. Did the Supreme Court have a bolt hole into which they could also escape? I couldn't imagine that they didn't. Our military had places which undoubtably survived intact, like the NORAD facility under Cheyenne Mountain in Colorado, and numerous hardened missile silos around the country.

Why had no attempt been made to contact the general public from these places? That was anyone's guess. When it became obvious that no secondary attack, from missiles for instance, was imminent, had the government elites come out of their shelters and been overwhelmed by starving crowds of looters? Had they attempted to rejoin their families, and been killed in the attempt? The possibilities were endless, but one thing was sure. The only way that civilization as we had known it could be re-established was to have communications, and that is exactly what Bernhard's orderly Swiss mind had realized. Thank God he had the will and resources to begin the process.

The discussions continued for another half hour. There was a growing awareness that because of our good fortune and extraordinary luck, we had an obligation to do what we could to reestablish order in the world, starting with our own nation. I assured the group that as I continued my discussions with Bernhard, I would keep them totally in the loop, not withholding anything. However, I also said that what was going to occur could not be governed by a committee rule. They must either trust me to act in their behalf, or choose another of our group as their leader. I looked around and saw nothing but shaking heads. It looked like I was stuck with that job, at least for now.

We closed the meeting and went into the Great Room for a glass of wine before dinner, which had been prepared by the gourmet chef cadre among our ladies. I took Ari and Jack Carson aside and told them I wanted them there when I had future conversations with Bernhard. They were, after all, my designated successors should anything happen to me. I told them I would take numerous aerial pictures of the Greenville-Spartanburg area when Bernhard arrived with his G-550 and we made the reconnaissance flight back to the Carolinas. Both Ari and Jack agreed that we would need the military perspective they both possessed if we decided to return to help, or perhaps evacuate, the Chimney Rock survivors.

After a good night's sleep and breakfast in the morning, Ari, Jack and I went to the radio room in the basement and contacted Bernhard on the scrambled shortwave radio. I told him that Ari and Jack were there with me, and why I felt that necessary. To my great relief, he heartily agreed with the concept, and said that he looked forward to meeting them personally on his arrival in Halifax. He also said to tell Dottie that he would bring his wife Genevieve with him. She had been used to traveling the world, and felt overly confined, never leaving Switzerland since the Event. I suspected she, like Dottie, wanted to protect the man in her life wherever she could, by inputting her thoughts and opinions as to plans and decisions being made. She and Bernhard, like Dottie and I, were mentally and emotionally "joined at the hip". I said it would be wonderful to see her, and asked which of the en-suite rooms they preferred, since they were basically all the same in this house. He said they always stayed on the top floor, to enjoy the view of the countryside and the ocean in the distance. I assured him a room would be prepared for their arrival. Mike and Kevin, who had been sharing one of the rooms, could move out to the bomb shelter, which indeed existed, again a near duplicate of the one at Bill's Mountain.

I asked Bernhard when he planned to make the trip, and how he planned to navigate all that distance with no GPS satellites available. He said the G-550 was now equipped with the "old fashioned" Internal Navigation Systems like we had on the original 747s. These require no external inputs, but are still very accurate. I was amazed he was able to find any under the circumstances. As to the timeframe, he said he hoped it would be in the next sixty days, before winter weather became a factor in North Carolina. It all depended on finishing the modifications on the Gulfstream. Everything was still quite unsettled in Switzerland, with the government raising and lowering the level of Marshal Law as the conditions dictated. Chaos still reigned in most of Europe, and the Swiss were standing alone against much of it.

While we waited, I decided that I must have further discussions with the authorities here in Halifax. They had been very accommodating so far, but were there limits to their benevolence towards our group? With that thought in mind, I called Mr. Lawrence and asked if he could set up a meeting with Inspector Walsh and any other official he thought might be appropriate. I also asked him if he was aware of Bernhard's plans for the future, and he assured me that he was, including the trip here from Switzerland, and the reconnaissance flight back to North Carolina. One thing more, he said, do not come armed to the meeting, or mention anything about the compound or it's armory. Interesting. Were the authorities aware of the weapons and turning a blind eye because of Bernhard's connections, or were they kept in the dark? That was something I would have to discuss with Bernhard when he arrived. For now, I assured Mr. Lawrence that "mums the word".

Currently, I felt that our group was living in some sort of undefined netherworld. Obviously, we weren't Canadian citizens, but were we Americans anymore either? Had national boundaries been extinguished along with all our electronic devices when the Event occurred? One thing was crystal clear to me. After all my years as a pilot, I needed a flight plan. Right now, I, along with the rest of us, was just making up the rules as I went along. That doesn't bode well for a successful flight or a stable existence. I needed a plan of attack. Perhaps in the next few days I would be able to begin to formulate one.

CHAPTER XXVIII

PLAN OF ATTACK

When one of the most severe CMEs occurred, the terminator was at approximately sixty-three and a half degree of longitude. It passed over Halifax and just a tiny bit of Prince Edward Island, plus virtually uninhabited portions of Quebec and Labrador and Newfoundland. To the best of my knowledge, no radio contact had been established with either Quebec or Labrador, and only very limited contact with Prince Edward Island. The rest of Canada was as silent as if it no longer existed. Unfortunately, the Canadian Parliament had been in session when the Event occurred, and most of the high-ranking Provincial officials had been attending a conference in Ottawa at the same time. That left only lower ranking, non-elected officials in the Province. Fortunately, Inspector Walsh was among them.

As it turned out, he was a personal friend of Mr. Lawrence, and a confidant of Bernhard Klaus. That fact made the meeting with him easier to set up, and much more candid and productive than might otherwise have been the case. Several days later I was advised that a meeting with Inspector Walsh had been scheduled for that Monday morning. I contacted Bernhard to advise him of that fact and he assured me that the discussion would be productive. He advised me to have an open mind, because he believed Inspector Walsh would divulge information unknown to me or our group and could be quite unsettling. He would say no more, even over what we believed to be a secure communications link. Once again, I was put in a situation where I had no idea what Bernhard was referring to. A disturbing pattern of events, but one I had learned to accept.

Over the weekend, I discussed my concerns with Ari, Dave Carson and Dottie. I felt that speaking to the whole group was inappropriate until I had more concrete information to pass on, and they agreed with my assessment. On Monday morning Mr. Lawrence sent a car to pick me up. As we drove through the countryside, I marveled at the beauty of the Nova Scotian fall. All the hardwood trees were turning from green to splashes of red, yellow and orange, made all the more dramatic by the background of dark green pine forests. I didn't speak to my driver during the forty-five-minute ride into Halifax, but sat alone with my thoughts.

We arrived at the Halifax City Hall Building, a very old and impressive structure, and as I stepped from the car I was met by Mr. Lawrence and Inspector Walsh, who then led me to a conference room on the first floor. Walsh closed the door behind him and walked to a large pull-down map of Canada. I noticed that there were several red dots on the map, mainly on Prince Edward Island and Labrador-New-foundland. On the mainland there were only a few, strangely in the middle of the country, In Manitoba and Saskatchewan Province's. Walsh picked up a wooden pointer and indicated these dots. "These are the only places we have been able to establish shortwave radio contact with since the EMP attack on our countries, and the CMEs that followed." He said. "You will note that I said 'Our Countries', since although the Iranians and North Koreans might have mainly targeted the United States, they must have been aware that the effect of the EMP weapons would also affect significant areas of Southern Canada and perhaps Northern Mexico as well." "The interior Province's contacts are Canadian Army and Air Force installations, while there is a mix of civilian and military contacts in our Maritime Province's."

I asked if there had been any contact with the Canadian Prime Minister or Parliament officials in Ottawa. "No, there have not, and that fact disturbs me greatly." He said. "One more thing. Our contacts with the military bases have been minimal. They refuse to share any information other than the basics. It is almost as if they have been instructed not to do so." "Why would that be the case?" I asked. "Considering the disaster which has befallen the world in general, and our countries in particular, you would assume that everyone would be working to restore order, including communications. It is incomprehensible to me that they wouldn't be working towards those goals." Walsh stared at his shoes for a long moment and looked up at me. "I don't understand either." He said. "I can only assume there is something going on with our government which they don't want to share on an insecure link for the time being." Mr. Lawrence now broke his silence. "I think I might have a clue." He said. "Mr. Klaus has described to you the chaos which exists in Europe at the present time." "He has come to the opinion that the Iranian government had planted sleeper cells in many countries in Europe and around the world, particularly North America, with instructions to start insurrections as soon as the EMP attacks were carried out on the United States. They couldn't have anticipated the severity of the CMEs, however, but still began their activities, even when they had no communications with the Iranian government. They probably still don't know about the retaliatory missile attacks the Americans carried out against Iran and North Korea. If they did, they might be even more fanatic in their efforts, like the "Twelvers" you encountered in North Carolina."

"Which brings us to the blackout of information from our government in Ottawa and the reluctance of our military installations to keep us in the loop." Said Inspector Walsh. "Canada, like much of Europe, had a large influx of Middle-Eastern immigrants for the last ten or twenty years, including a significant number from Iran and Iranian allies. Did they rise up after the EMP attack and slaughter our government officials in a pre-planned attack?" "That action is all too possible, considering what has occurred, or more to the point NOT occurred over the last eighteen months."

The implications of that concept swept over me like a tidal wave. Had this happened in Washington as well? Were our Federal officials overwhelmed when they left the safety of their bunkers when it became evident that a nuclear attack wasn't on the way after the EMPs and CMEs? Was that why there hadn't been communications or guidance from our government? Had it simply ceased to exist, and if so, who was now in control of our major cities? The answers to those and other questions were unobtainable, at least for now, but it was becoming clear to me that Bernhard's plan to begin to rebuild our societies from the ground up made more and more sense. The question was, would one very wealthy Swiss business man, even with the resources available to him, have the means and will to accomplish these tasks? Walsh had a light lunch delivered to our conference room, and we continued our discussions until late that afternoon.

Mr. Lawrence and Walsh agreed with the concept of our reconnaissance flight back to the Carolinas as a start. We were all aware that Bernhard Klaus being physically present was essential to any further discussions or plans. His arrival from Switzerland would put in motion a series of events which could indeed lead to the resurrection of civilization on the planet. Until that time, we must decide how much information we could or should share with others outside this tiny inner circle. I stated flat out that I must keep Ari, Jack and Dottie in the loop, and they both agreed. Inspector Walsh said that he wanted to introduce me to several other people he felt should be part of the team we were putting together, specifically, the Harbormasters of Yarmouth and Halifax, the head of the air traffic system at the Halifax airport, the Director of the Nova Scotia Water Management Agency and the Managing Director of the Dartmouth Oil Refinery among others. How much information we shared with them initially would be decided by the three of us until Bernhard arrived. None of us had a desire to plan in secret, but there were just too many possibilities of something going wrong if the wrong people misinterpreted our plans and goals and spread false information to an already jittery population. Winston Churchill once said that "In wartime, truth is so precious that she should always be attended by a bodyguard of lies". We were surely in a war for our very survival, so a little prevarication on our part would have to be acceptable under the circumstances.

I returned to the compound that afternoon to discover that the promised fleet of SUVs for our use had arrived. To lessen the tensions and anxieties which still existed among the group, I suggested that we take a few day trips to see the Province, packing lunches for the sightseeing excursions. In this way, we were slowly transformed from refugees who had only recently escaped unimaginable danger and violence, to tourists in a strange but lovely place. None of us had ever spent any time in Nova Scotia or any of the other Canadian Maritime Province's. I had been of the impression that it was an island Province like Prince Edward Island and Newfoundland. However, when I had a chance to study the local road maps, I discovered that it indeed was a peninsula of the mainland, attached by a narrow neck of land to New Brunswick Provence. This then begged the question of why had there been no movement of Canadians to one of the few areas of the country, or the world for that matter, which still had a functional power grid and some semblance of a normal society. When I asked Inspector Walsh that question, he replied that the area around the boundary between the Province's had not been in the Terminator protected zone, and as such all communications with it had been lost. The Nova

Scotian officials who remained in charge had decided to close Canadian Route 104 south of Spring Hill, and closely monitored the area after hearing what had occurred in Europe and the United States from Bernhard Klaus. It had become a dead zone, with no traffic in either direction for over a year. That was a long way from Halifax, and our sightseeing excursions never went beyond a two-hour drive from the compound so the mystery of non-communication with New Brunswick remained just that, a mystery.

As October passed into November, our explorations ceased as the weather grew increasingly colder. Then, two events occurred. Suzi Mason gave birth to a beautiful baby girl on November ninth, the delivery expertly handled by Peggy Fleming and Janet Lewis. The following day, we heard from Bernhard Klaus. The modifications on his airplane had been completed, and he would be arriving the following Monday, less than a week later. Planning for the return flight to North Carolina would begin, with the flight hopefully completed by the end of the month.

CHAPTER XXIX

THE RETURN

The week flew by. I spent much of the time on the radio with Bernhard, discussing what we should try to parachute drop to the survivors on Chimney Rock. It would do no good to provide them with walkie-talkies, as I had dropped to Megan from the J-3 Cub over the Bill's Mountain compound. The jet noise and speed would make communications difficult with those, if not impossible. It was determined that the best choice would be handheld battery powered VHF radios with instructions how to use them. In addition, we would supply them with several battery powered shortwave radios, again with instructions as to how to rig antennas to give them the range to converse with us in Nova Scotia. Bernhard informed us that he would bring all these radios, plus an additional stock with him from Switzerland. In addition, he would bring specially designed parachutes to drop the equipment over Chimney Rock. We had of course no contact with those people for over two months, and could only hope they were still safe in their mountain enclave.

Ari and Jack Swanson drew lots to determine who would be on the reconnaissance flight with me. Ari won. He would be able to view the entire area from a military perspective, take many photographs, and then consult with Jack when we returned as to our best options to help the Chimney Rock survivors, and perhaps other groups in the area. Our initial goal was to begin to fill in some of the blanks in our knowledge of what had happen to our country since the Event. Right now, those blanks far exceeded any concrete information available.

On Monday afternoon I got a call from Mr. Lawrence. That's how he always identified himself when he called. I guess he felt that first name basis was reserved for very few, certainly not for acquaintances of only a couple of months. I wondered if he was also Swiss. He said that the tower at the Halifax Airport had just received a call from Bernhard's plane. They expected to arrive in about twenty-five minutes. I immediately gathered Ari, Jack and Dottie and drove to the airport. Bernhard's Gulfstream was on its final approach when we arrived at the field and drove to the General Aviation area where Klaus's Halifax hangar was located. We were all standing there on the ramp, accompanied by Lawrence and Inspector Walsh, when the big business jet taxied up to the hangar and shut down its engines. After a moment or two, the cabin door opened, and there in the doorway stood Bernhard Klaus. He didn't look a day older than the last time I saw him, over four years earlier. Behind him as he came down the steps was his wife Genevieve, smartly dressed as usual. She immediately embraced Dottie, and then gave me a big hug as well. She, like Bernhard, was fully aware that my actions in New Mexico had surely saved her life, and she never forgot that fact. Bernhard gave me a firm handshake, and then turned to do the same to Walsh, Lawrence, and then Ari and Jack, as I introduced them. "It was a long flight. We both need to rest a bit before dinner". He said. "Robert and John, you must join us for dinner, we have much to discuss." That was the first time I had heard Inspector Walsh's first name, but obviously he, as was the case with Lawrence, was on a first name basis with Bernhard.

At six o'clock that evening the eight of us met for dinner at the home of John Lawrence, which was a large house overlooking a fantastic view of cliffs and the Atlantic Ocean several miles north of Halifax proper. Bernhard stipulated this location because it was secure, and he wanted to share what he had to say with a limited number of people. More of his penchant for security, but I had grown used to that.

He stood at the head of the table and raised a wine glass in a toast. "To the survival of the Water Lily Warriors." He said. "And to the rebirth of civilization on our planet." We all raised our glasses in agreement, and he continued. "Let us enjoy our meal in peace, and then I will tell you what I have in mind." We did so, just making small talk while an excellent meal of Nova Scotian seafood, including a mussel appetizer, a wonderful seafood chowder and two pound lobsters were consumed with relish by us all. After dessert and coffee was finished, we repaired to the study, and Bernard once again began to speak. "As I have told you, Europe is in chaos, the rest of the world as well, from what I have been able to learn by talking to survivors in various of my secure compounds around the globe. I built them to protect against a nuclear war and its aftermath. There was no way I could have imagined what was actually going to befall our planet." He began. "The almost total breakdown of civilized society in the aftermath of the EMP attacks on North America and the CMEs, which devastated most of the rest of the planet, is almost beyond comprehension, although it was accurately predicted by a scientific study done in the United States early in this century." "The question is, what can we do about it? Are we doomed as a species to extinction?"

He slowly turned his head and looked us individually in the eyes. "I think not, or perhaps I should say I hope not, but no time can be wasted in an attempt to start putting things right, to reestablishing order, and to rebuilding civilized societies around the globe." "Since it was thrust into the role of the leader of the free world after the end of the Second World War, the United States has been the example to all nations of what a truly free people can aspire to. It wasn't perfect, but it gave hope to many people who had previously known nothing but oppression, that there was a better way of life." "What got in the way was politics and politicians." "Especially in the U.S.," "If they had paid attention to the extensive report produced by their EMP Commission, and took steps to harden the power grid, communications facilities and military installations, we might not be where we are today."

"So, what is my plan?" "I believe that the Bill's Mountain compound, if it has not been destroyed by vengeful Iranian 'Twelvers', can be a base for the projects I will explain later in greater detail." "I brought over ten thousand pounds of freeze dried foods in Mylar packets with me. These will be distributed to the Chimney Rock survivors, and others as required. You can't fight on an empty stomach, and as you are all well aware, the Iranians are still in the area in significant numbers, and assumedly well-armed." "I have other disturbing news. Apparently, part of the plans developed and implemented by the Iranian Mullahs was to supply and distribute ground to air missiles, to disrupt air travel, to their various cells worldwide," "They meant them to be used to shoot down commercial airliners, but can be fired at any aircraft they choose." "I would guess that they didn't think the Piper Cubs were worthy targets, and the C-47 was only used after your attack on the compound, which I am sure totally disrupted their operational capabilities." "However, they must have regrouped since you escaped, and the missiles, if they have them, could be a threat to our reconnaissance flight and future supply or rescue missions." "However, " he continued "I have good news in that area." "One of the modifications I accomplished on the Gulfstream was to install an anti-missile defense system similar to those reportedly installed on all El Al airliners, Air Force One and many nations military aircraft. That should protect us from that type of attack."

Bernhard also stated that he had brought twenty pair of handheld VHF radios and twenty pair of battery powered shortwave transceivers, plus twenty solar powered units which could recharge the radios batteries when they were depleted. Again, it appeared he had thought this through very thoroughly, in typical Klaus fashion. If we succeeded, I was sure there would be statues of Bernhard Klaus erected worldwide to honor the savior of civilization. He said that he needed several days to adjust to the time zone, and then we would depart on our flight back to Chimney Rock. That ended the evening, and we all returned to the compound. The planning would continue in the morning.

It did. I decided to call for a meeting of the entire group, where I outlined Bernhard's plans, both for the initial reconnaissance flight back to the Carolinas, and then for a possible return to the area to help other survivors and reestablish a lawful society. That statement brought a mixed reaction. Some, mainly the older members, just shook their heads in disbelief. Go back? Into that maelstrom of danger and uncertainty? Especially since we had escaped to a place of evident safety and security? Was I mad? Others however, particularly Dave and Joyce Carson, Jack and Karen Swanson, Ari and Rachael Zuckerman, my son Michael and his friend Kevin Landry, nodded in agreement. I looked carefully at Megan and Matt and Bill and Suzi Mason. They had children to consider, in the case of the Masons, a newborn baby. Frankly, they just looked bewildered, and I could understand why. Nothing had to be decided now, however, and I made that abundantly clear to all.

Later in the morning, Bernhard and Genevieve joined us. They both looked refreshed after a good night's sleep. After they had their breakfast, Bernhard joined Ari, Dave and me for a planning session. We determined that we would drop the VHF and shortwave radios in two separate packages, one each in both. They would be securely wrapped in soft foam rubber and an outer shell of Styrofoam to absorb the impact of the landing. In this way, even if one package was lost or damaged, we should be able to communicate with them on the other. The parachutes were basically just slightly larger versions of the drogue chutes used to pull the main chute out of a sky divers main chute pack. We planned to drop them at about two hundred feet above Chimney Rock, so wind currents wouldn't blow them off course into the valley below, presumably occupied by the Iranians. In addition, in two separate packages, we would drop two thousand freeze dried Mylar meal packets and several hundred bottles of antibiotic tablets. We would find out their other needs when communications were established. The flight was scheduled two days hence.

The night before we left, Bernhard, Dave, Ari and I ate a private dinner in the dining room, accompanied by our wives. Dottie, Rachael and Genevieve were plainly nervous. Their husbands were going in harm's way, with an uncertain outcome. Did the Iranians who survived my attack with the Corsair indeed have surface to air missiles at their disposal, and would the anti-missile technology installed on the Gulfstream protect it if they did? That was plainly an unknown. If it didn't, the mission would end in tragedy, and we were all aware of that fact. None of this was part of the dinner conversations, but it lay like an invisible shroud over the evening. Tomorrow would be another do or die event, and we all knew it.

Dottie slept with me in a single queen-sized bed, something she rarely did these days, as I tossed and turned frequently while I slept. She snuggled extra close that night, with her arm around my waist. This might be our last night together on this earth, and after fifty years of marriage, we loved each other deeply. I guess she symbolically didn't want to let go. Long after she drifted off to sleep, I listened to her softly snoring, and with that wonderful white noise to cancel out my tinnitus, I finally fell asleep as well. Tomorrow was going to be a long and eventful day.

As agreed, we were up and out by seven the next morning. We drove to the airport in silence. When we arrived at the hangar, the airplane had already been pulled out onto the ramp. We went into the flight planning room, and all shook hands with Helmut Schmidt, Bernhard's pilot. He showed me what was planned. Basically, he had programed the known latitude and longitude of the Bill's Mountain compound into the INS units on the Gulfstream. He knew that I was familiar with their use, since I had used similar models for years on the Lockheed 1011s and Boeing 747s I had flown for Trans World Airlines prior to my retirement. They required no external inputs, and would allow us to easily reach our destination and return to Halifax. The fuel tanks had been topped off, and we had more than enough fuel onboard to complete the mission several times over. All planned cargo had been securely tied down in the cabin, and the rear mounted drop chute checked for proper operation. The one factor we could not plan for was the en route and destination weather information, as all those reporting services had ceased when the Event and CMEs had destroyed almost all of the global electronics. We could only hope for the best.

We were airborne at nine-fifteen, with a planned flight time of less than two hours, compared with the over nine hours required to cover the same distance in the C-47. Thankfully, the autumn skies were clear for the full route, much of it over water. We were cruising at thirty-nine thousand feet, and it felt wonderful to be sitting in the cockpit of a modern jet aircraft once again, after all these years. Helmut kindly allowed me to occupy the left seat of the Gulfstream, the position where he normally would have sat as pilot-in-command of the flight. "Why don't you fly the leg." He said. "Since you are more familiar with the area than I am." I eagerly agreed, and felt all the old procedures return. Since the INS groundspeed indicator showed we had about a fifty mile an hour headwind, I waited until we were about a hundred miles out to begin our descent from cruise altitude. It was a beautifully clear day here as well, and it was hard to believe things weren't perfectly normal below us. Towns, cities and many airports were visible below along our route after we came back onshore in Northern Virginia. However, no smoke rose from any of the power plants we saw, including several nuclear ones. Normally, on a cool fall day, there would be dense clouds of steam rising from the plants cooling towers. I could only assume that the backup power of the plants had allowed the reactors to be shut down after the Event, or a Chernobyl style meltdown and explosion would have occurred as soon as the un-replenished cooling waters evaporated around the core. There was no visible evidence of that.

We decided to approach Chimney Rock from the opposite direction of the Iranian compound, making several low passes to attract the attention of the survivors below, before we dropped the radios and food supplies. The downside of that was that we would also surely attract the attention of the Iranians and their possible ground to air missiles. Unfortunately, that couldn't be avoided. We would just have to be extremely careful and vigilant. Captain Schmidt continued to allow me to fly the plane, and I made a wide sweeping turn just south of Asheville, aiming toward Lake Lure and Chimney Rock, which I could see in the distance as I descended. My first pass was at what I estimated to be two hundred feet and at an indicated speed of nearly three-hundred and fifty knots. I immediately turned sharply to the right, away from the valley to our left, and set up for another low altitude, high speed pass over the rock. That accomplished, I again turned to the right and began to slow down to a speed where we could open the rear dump chute and drop the parachutes over the rock. That would entail drastically slowing to flap extension speed, extending several degrees of flaps, and then slowing to one hundred and fifty knots. This was when we would be most vulnerable to attack from a missile or even automatic rifle fire from below. As I slowed to drop speed, Ari and Bernhard prepared for the first drop. We depressurized the cabin and gave them the signal to lower the chute. That done, I set up on the first run, and just before Chimney Rock passed under the nose, we told them to throw out the chutes. I then again banked hard right and prepared for the second drop. Ari said he and Bernhard were ready, and the run began. The second load was away when I heard a loud screeching noise in my headset. "That's the missile alarm from the anti-missile system! They've launched a missile at us. Bank hard right and accelerate!" Schmidt said. "I'll retract the flaps and raise the dump chute. Max power! NOW!" I did so, and seconds later we felt an explosion shake the airplane. The anti-missile system had worked, but it was a one-shot deal. We had to get out of range as quickly as possible or we were dead men.

I accelerated to maximum speed and then began a rapid climb to an altitude which was above the maximum height a man-pad missile could reach. That was close call, and we all knew it. Leveling out at twenty-four thousand feet, I continued a turn to a course parallel to the valley below Chimney Rock. "A flag!" Schmidt said. "I can see a large American flag on a pole atop the rock!" So, they were still there. They had seen and heard us. Hopefully, the radios and food were in their hands, and they soon would be calling on the VHF transceivers. We continued our climb to thirty-seven thousand feet, the altitude we would cruise on the way back to Halifax and then waited for a transmission from below as we orbited overhead. After about twenty minutes, it came in loud and clear. "Can you hear us?" The voice said. "Who are you?" "Hopefully, your salvation." I replied. "We can't stay long, but we'll be back. Glad to hear your voice and that you've survived up there." "Did the other radios land undamaged?" I asked." "Yeah, everything is okay. We got all four parachute bundles." Came the reply. "Well read the documentation, and rig the shortwave antenna as directed. People are waiting to hear from you. We have to leave now, but as I said, we'll be back. Over and out."

Bernhard and Ari came up and we all shook hands. "I took over a hundred pictures of the area, including the Iranian compound valley." Ari said. "That was close. I hope we can re-arm the anti-missile defense system when we get back to Halifax. I don't think that was the only rocket those bastards have down there." "We can." Bernhard replied. We came well equipped from Lausanne." We programmed the Halifax coordinates into the INS units and headed back. We had completed our mission and survived unscathed. Our next steps would be the topic of discussion when we got back to Nova Scotia, but it was a good beginning.

CHAPTER XXX

THE BREAKUP

On our arrival back in Halifax we were met at the airport by Dave Carson and our wives. They were plainly greatly relieved to see that we had returned unharmed from the reconnaissance. We returned to the compound and enjoyed a wonderful dinner for the whole group, this prepared by a local chef Bernhard had engaged to cook a special meal which included many local delicacies including mussels, clams and oysters from the ocean, and roast Moose, something none of us had ever tasted. It was declared delicious by all. After the meal, as we sat around sipping an after-dinner glass of brandy or port from Bernhard's excellent cellar, he stood up and said he would like to call a group meeting for the following afternoon. It was time, he declared, to determine where we would go from here, and he wanted everyone to ponder that thought until tomorrow. We all looked at each other, and in silence went up to bed.

At the appointed hour we all filed into the entertainment room and sat in the semi-circular, tiered rows which made up the small amphitheater. On the giant TV screen, there was a Mercator projection map of the world, with a series of vertical lines drawn through it at irregular intervals. I studied it briefly and determined that it must show where the various terminator shielded areas, and as such normal electronic communication still existed. They were pitifully small. Bernhard stood to one side, and with a laser pointer to indicate various points of interest, began to speak.

"These are the areas where some form of normalcy still exists, from what I and my staff in Lausanne have been able to determine. You will note that no part of Switzerland is among them." He began. "However, much of the Swiss infrastructure was protected from the effects the CMEs because they were located in artificial caverns excavated by our government for self-defense purposes or were in artificially hardened above ground structures that we had mandated some years back, when the threat of EMPs were first discussed. Most of Switzerland is therefore fully functional. Unfortunately, the rest of the European Continent was not so well prepared. A state of chaos exists virtually everywhere else in Europe, and that is true for most of the rest of the globe as well. Your horrific experiences over the last eighteen months and more, have become the norm, not a rarity. It falls to us then, the fortunate few, to either barricade ourselves against those who would take what we still have, or do whatever is in our power to help restore order and civilization on our planet. That will be an enormous task, and will probably not be accomplished in the lifetimes of most of us in this room because of our age.

But for the sake of the younger generations, also represented here, and THEIR children, we must try. At least we must begin the process."

He gazed at us all for a moment and then continued. "I have a broad outline in my mind as to HOW to begin, but I must know who amongst this group are willing to once again put their lives on the line and return to America, to the Carolinas, and begin the process." "We have heard from the Chimney Rock survivors over the shortwave radios we provided yesterday. They are in desperate need of food, medical supplies, arms and ammunition. The only reason they have not been overwhelmed by lawless looters or the murderous Iranian Twelvers, is because they hold a nearly impregnable position on the top of the mountain above Chimney Rock. There are only a few narrow pathways up there, which are easily defended. But as I said, they are running out of about everything they require to survive. Winter is coming, and they haven't been able to replenish anything for months. Our arrival was a Godsend to them."

"So now, it is time to decide." Bernhard continued. "After all you have gone through, no one will think less of you if you choose to remain here in Nova Scotia, but I must have a show of hands as to who is willing to go back, and try to restore order in your country." Of the original twenty Water Lily Warriors, only fourteen were left. Five had been cruelly murdered by Iranian Twelver fanatics and the sixth, a turncoat who participated in four of those deaths was killed by me as he threatened Dottie's life. The final six people who made it to the supposed safety of the Bill's Mountain compound were much younger, and four of them had young children to care

223

for. Slowly, eleven hands were raised. I looked around me, not surprised at who was volunteering with one exception, and that was young Bill Mason.

I stood up and began to speak to the group I had led for most of the last two years. I had a lump in my throat as I started. "I have to go back." I said. "Not as an act of courage, we have all demonstrated that many times over since the Event. I have to return because I believe Bernhard is right. We must try to restore order and peace to the planet, and America has always been a leader in that endeavor." "I see that my dear wife has also raised her hand, but I won't try to speak for her. She can explain her decision herself." I sat down and Dottie arose and looked around at the others. "I agree with Al." She said. "But that's not why I raised my hand. We have been together for over fifty years, sharing good times and bad, triumphs and failures, but thankfully no great tragedies. We have grown to share a personality, and indeed sometimes I think, a brain!" She looked up at me and smiled as she reached out and grasped my hand. "I demanded to be his observer when we flew in Water Lily One because I wanted to be with him, whatever happened. We are indeed joined at the hip mentally and spiritually. As our wedding vow proclaimed, 'til death do us part'."

My son Michael was next to stand. "I'm single." He said. "I don't have anyone to worry about but me." "I think dad and Mr. Klaus are right. If civilization is to be saved, we are the ones to get the ball rolling, and I want one more chance to settle the score with those Twelvers." Kevin Landry was next. "I'm an Aussie, but America is my adopted home. It's treated me well, and I want to return the favor." Then Ari and

Rachael Zuckerman stood together. "I was born in Israel." Said Ari. "Through my marriage to Rachael I gained American citizenship. I also owe that country a great deal. I hope the spark of freedom and safety we start in the Carolinas will spread worldwide, to my original homeland as well." Rachael just nodded in silent agreement.

Next up was Dave and Joyce Carson. "I agree with Al once again." "I remember a saying attributed to John F. Kennedy. 'If not us, who? If not now, when?' Joyce and I talked it over last night and agreed we have to go back and try to help those people who were left behind. It's as simple as that."

Jack Swanson rose and said "I was a high school history teacher for most of my career. I remember trying to instill in my students the concepts of historical right and wrong. The inevitable triumph of right over might. This is a classic example of that concept to Karen and me. We must go back and fight against the evil which has befallen our country and our planet. That's all I have to say."

Finally, Bill Mason stood up. "I'm not much for talk." He said. "Only got a high school education." "But now that I know what happened to my country was a deliberate act, committed by a bunch of crazy bastards that are still out there killing innocent people, I have to try to stop that. What kind of world will our baby grow up in if I don't? Suzi's got to stay here and take care of the baby."

Dale Lawrence stood up. "I know that for the entire time since the Event occurred Harriet and I were basically just go-fers for the group. Coming from Long Island New York, we were just getting used to living in a house in Happy Valley instead of a high-rise apartment. We will do anything we can to support your efforts, but I think we'd be more of a hindrance than a help. We have decided to remain in Nova Scotia and make a life here if the Canadians will accept us as part of the community.

Next came Peggy Fleming. "I have checked with the hospitals here in Nova Scotia, and they are all critically short of skilled nurses." "Bill and I have talked this over with Dan and Janet Lewis. We've both decided to stay here and help out. We respect all you've done for us, but hope you'll understand our decision."

Finally, my daughter Megan stood up and motioned for Matt to stand with her. "This is really tough for me daddy, but I have asked Matt to remain here with me, at least for the time being. We have our daughters, your granddaughters, to consider. What would happen to them if God forbid, they lost their parents. You know I love you and mom, but I just can't go back, I just can't." She said with a sob. "Please forgive me." Dottie walked over and took her in her arms. "It's okay honey, it's okay." She said.

Bernhard nodded. "I understand your reasons for remaining here, and as I said, no one will think less of you." "Now, we will have a day of rest and reflection. Tomorrow, those of you who have volunteered to return must join me as we plan a "Reconquista". If you have never heard that term, I will explain it in detail when we next meet.

So, that was the breakup of the Water Lily Warriors. There were hugs and kind words all around. We had gone through more that most of us could have comprehended prior to the Event, and we would never forget each other for as long as we lived.

EPILOGUE

RECONQUISTA AMERICA

After defeating the Visigoths in North Africa, the Moors, as Muslims were known at the time, crossed the Straits of Gibraltar in 711 AD and invaded the Iberian Peninsula. They expanded their territory northward for the next twenty years, and invaded Southern France in early 732 AD. Their goal was to capture and sack Paris. At the Battle of Tours in October of that year the Frankish leader Charles Martel defeated the Moorish army under Emir Abdul Rahman Al Ghafiqi Abd al Rahman, killing him, and driving the Moors back into Spain where they remained for the next seven hundred years.

The Spanish "Reconquista" (recapture) began in the twelfth century and continued, gradually driving the Moorish forces south from previously conquered Spanish territory until they were finally driven back across the Straits of Gibraltar in 1492.

This was the goal set forth by Bernhard Klaus in our meeting the next morning after the breakup. His plan basically entailed resupplying the Chimney Rock survivors by air drops with food, medical supplies, guns and ammunition. Then, with their help, securing the Greenville-Spartanburg Airport, using that as a base to defeat the Iranian Twelver compound, which had terrorized the region since the EMP attack on North America. That accomplished, we would contact other survivors in the area, and expand our area of operations as quickly as possible. Any remaining looters must be ruthlessly wiped out, and law enforcement reestablished.

How would we do this? That was the question. Was it even possible? "Well," I pondered out loud. "Who would have thought that a group of senior citizens with entirely different backgrounds, living in a retirement community in South Carolina, could come together, against unspeakable odds and adversity, and using whatever implements and equipment they had at hand, defeat a series of deadly adversaries, and not only survive, but prosper?" "Ingenuity and WILL are what we need to take back our state, then our region, country, continent and hopefully the entire planet, someday in the distant future. By that time, the Water Lily Warriors will probably just be a distant memory, but a memory of a bunch of seniors who were SURVIVORS. Who would never give up, NEVER."

"Enough talk!" I finally said loudly at the end of our planning meeting with Bernhard. "Let's get going!" And we did.

End of Book One

GLOSSARY

ADF - **A**utomatic **D**irection **F**inder - An early form of radio navigation. It will point to a radio station which is transmitting in the low to mid frequency bands.

AGL - A flying term abbreviation for **A**bove **G**round **L**evel at your current location.

AR-15 - A semi-automatic rifle often mis-identified as an "Assault Rifle" because of its resemblance to the military M-16 fully automatic weapon. It comes in several calibers, and is a favorite of many "preppers" for self-defense and hunting purposes.

ATC - Air Traffic Control. These are the people who man ground control, the tower, approach and departure radar and the various "ATC Center Radar facilities" which control the airspace across the country.

AWOS - Automated Weather Observation Service. These computer operated weather stations are available at many controlled and uncontrolled airports around the country. They are required at any airport which has a published instrument approach, to give the pilot information about required ceiling and visibility.

CB - "Citizens Band" radios which are commonly used by truckers for social talk or advice about road conditions. Sometimes used by average drivers who do a lot of long-distance travel.

CME - Coronal mass ejection. This is an ejection of plasma from the sun that sends highly charged particles into space, including directly towards Earth. It is a very large Solar Flare, and depending on the position of the event in relation to Earth, the effects can vary and can mimic an EMP in many ways. A very large one, or a series of them, could almost drive our planet back to the days before the electronic equipment we use every day existed.

DME - Distance Measuring Equipment. An aircraft system which measures and indicates the distance from a transmitter in tenth of a mile segment.

EMP - Electromagnetic Pulse. A pulse generated anytime a thermonuclear explosion occurs. EMPs can cause severe damage to various electronic components, especially the "chips" which allow the functioning of many everyday items like automobiles, cellphones, computers, televisions and radios.

EMT - Emergency Medical Technician. These people are trained above a level of first aid, but below that of Registered Nurses. They are what are generally staff ambulances, and one will be part of the medical crew in an air ambulance, along with a Flight Nurse who is an R/N, and occasionally a doctor if the case is serious enough.

Glock - A well-known brand of semi-automatic handgun first designed and manufactured in Austria; it is now also manufactured in the U.S. as well. It comes in various calibers, and is favored by many law enforcement agencies worldwide.

Ground Effect - The effect of added aerodynamic buoyancy produced by a cushion of air below an aircraft moving close to the ground or water.

GSP - The airport identifier for the Greenville-Spartanburg International Airport in Greer, SC.

IFR - Instrument Flight Rules. Flying an aircraft partially or solely by the use of flight instruments. Although helicopters can do this, the reality is that they rarely do.

ILS - Instrument Landing System. Used for low visibility approaches and landings.

Laager - A system of circling wagons into a defensive ring to ward off the possibility of a surprise attack, especially at night. It was devised by Dutch "Afrikaner" speaking Boers for safety during their "treks" into the South African interior to find new arable land in the 19th century.

Man-Pad - A shoulder fired ground to air missile similar to the American "Stinger" missile and others manufactured by various nations around the world.

Mauser - A famous brand of German rifle, renowned for its accuracy and durability.

MDA - Minimum Descent Altitude. The lowest an aircraft is authorized to descend during a non-precision approach until the approach lights or runway lights are visible.

MRE - Meal Ready to Eat. Pre-packaged military meals. The successors to the C-Rations and K-Rations of earlier military generations.

NDB - **N**on-**D**irectional **B**eacon - A low frequency radio transmitter used by aircraft for radio navigation, using their "ADF" receiver.

"Prepper" - This term is applied, often in a derogatory fashion, to those who feel that it is necessary to prepare for the unexpected. Something as simple as a short-term power outage caused by an ice storm or hurricane, or as disastrous as an indefinite cessation of government services, food and water supplies by something like an EMP attack on our country. Preppers buy and stock long-life freeze-dried food supplies, water filtration equipment, and other survival gear. The "preppers" in this story are the ones who have allowed the group to have a chance for survival after an unimaginable event transpired. They are not believers in "End of the World" scenarios, but simply people who have paid attention, and studied what happened to individuals who were unprepared when events like Hurricane Katrina occurred.

Satcom - A satellite communications device resembling a large telephone or a small radio.

Travois - A type of sledge formerly used by North American Indians to carry goods, consisting of two joined poles pulled by a horse or dog. The "trekkers" in our story have designed a modernized version, using bicycle wheels on an axle, and pulled by human walkers.

UHF - Ultra-High Frequency radios. Typically used by the military for air to air and air to ground communication.

VHF - Very-High Frequency radios. Normally used for civilian air to ground

communication.

VOR – Very High Frequency Omni-Directional Range. A commonly used ground based navigational system used mainly by civilian aircraft.

**Enjoy this prologue
of D.A. Francis's
second book,
*A Rock and a Hard Place:
The Return of the Warriors.***

PROLOGUE

NIGHT IN THE DESERT

Pablo was shivering. Anyone who thought the desert in Northern Mexico was always warm had never been there in the winter months. Even though it was late March, the daytime temperatures rarely reached eighty degrees, and the desert rapidly gave up its heat after sunset. By now, about one in the morning, the thermometer hovered just above freezing, and a brisk wind made it feel even colder.

The trucks carrying the shipment had stopped five miles south of the border, and the unloading and reloading process had begun. Pablo wasn't sure what the crates contained as they were loaded on the backs of the little donkeys who awaited their arrival at midnight, but he was pretty certain it wasn't drugs, the normal cargo his band of "Coyotes" smuggled across the border into Arizona. The boxes were made of sturdy wood, held together with metal straps. They had words stenciled on the top, but since Pablo couldn't read Spanish, let alone English, he didn't know what they said.

The Iranians who had contracted with the cartel to smuggle these items safely into the United States had specified that the men who comprised this particular smuggling crew had to be two things: illiterate and expendable. So, as the little caravan walked along the narrow path through the canyon towards the border, now only several miles away, the clients of the cartel had basically three thoughts in mind: Getting to the vans, which had been pre-positioned two miles north of this basically unprotected stretch of the border, loading the crates into them, and eliminating the witnesses. All this must be accomplished before dawn.

Crossing the border was a non-event. They simply cut the three-strand barbed wire fence and walked through. There were no lights visible at that hour, and the Coyotes knew that they were at least a mile and a half from any building north of the border. They covered the final segment in less than an hour, and just as promised, three Ford panel vans awaited them. After loading the wooden crates from the twelve donkeys into the vans, the smugglers stood in a line, waiting for the cash tip that was customary.

They couldn't have expected what happened next. The customers closed the back doors of the vans and slowly turned to face the smugglers. Each held a compact "Uzi" sub-machine gun that had been concealed under their down jackets. These lethal little weapons, although manufactured by the hated "Little Satan", Israel, were among the finest of their type manufactured anywhere on the planet.

It was over in seconds. All six Coyotes and their twelve little donkeys lay dead on the ground, riddled with bullets. The three Iranians gave a high five to each other, got in the vans, and drove off into the night. There was just a hint of dawn on the eastern horizon. They would be well into the State of Texas before they stopped for the night at a small compound owned by a sleeper cell of fellow Iranians. The wooden crates were transferred to three large SUVs. In the morning, these vehicles would begin the rest of their journey east, ending up at their Mosque in South Carolina two days hence. The crates would be transferred one more time. Security was tight, but Inshallah, all would go well. The Ayatollah would be pleased.

Ninety-three million miles away, just below the surface of the Sun, a disturbance was forming. There had not been one this large in the recorded history of mankind, but many others, even larger, had occurred in the four and a half billion year history of the planet. This one would change everything.

ABOUT THE AUTHOR

Like Captain Al Farragut, one of the main characters, and the narrator of this novel, the author is a retired international airline Captain, who spent more than 36 years flying for one of the world's most famous airlines. He has been flying since his teens, and like Farragut, flew for an air ambulance company after retiring from the airline. He and his wife Dottie lived for nine years in a large retirement community in South Carolina's Low Country before moving west to the foothills of the Blue Ridge Mountains. He is also a "prepper", and extremely concerned about the lack of preparedness to deal with the many threats to our country that exist today.